# The Strength Of St. Croix

### By Tom Sedar

© 2024

Books in the St. Croix Mystery Series

The Gold of St. Croix

The Snow of St. Croix

The Strength of St. Croix

The King of St. Croix (set for publication in April of 2024)

For previews of upcoming books by Tom Sedar and more information about the author,

Visit: www.tomsedar.com

The Strength of St. Croix

# THE STRENGTH OF ST. CROIX

## BY

## TOM SEDAR

## CHAPTER 1

**MANY THINGS ON THE ISLAND OF ST. CROIX ARE MUCH MORE AND MUCH LESS THAN THEY APPEAR.**

My name is Mad Dog Cotton, and the island of St. Croix is my home. Like most islands in the tropics, it is hot if the winds aren't blowing. It was early August, and the trade winds off the Caribbean were dead.

I was sitting at Ziggy's, the local east-end gas station, fighting the afternoon heat with a combination of shade and ice-cold beer. My wife Cheri, our partner Ray Jones, and I work together as private investigators. It's never been a job any of us planned, and we don't advertise or even have an office. The best way to describe it is when people on the island have a problem, they seem to come to us.

Cheri, Ray, and I had come to Ziggy's for gas. To our dismay, the gas station was out of gas. In classic St. Croix style, the gas station did have a hell of a beer special. I parked my truck while Ray and Cheri bought three ice-cold Elephant beers and claimed three chairs in the shade at the little bar built onto the side of the gas station.

In some parts of the civilized world, the area we sat in would not have qualified as a bar. But it had all the prerequisites. It had an eight-foot length of unfinished plywood cut in half, which of course formed the "bar." It had the required bartender, a bearded gentleman whose age could have ranged from a spry seventy to a well warn fifty. It had two large beer coolers filled with beer, coke, and lots of ice. It had a gallon of Cruzan light rum and a gallon of Cruzan dark rum sitting on the ground beside the beer coolers, and last, but not least, it had a metal box to put the money in. Who says you can't start a business for a hundred bucks or less?

I forgot, it also had a boom box at the end of the bar, Zac Brown crooning about his feet, sand, and of course beer.

As I sipped my second one-dollar Elephant Lager, I ignored the deep and important conversation that Ray and Cheri had dropped into. Normally, I would have been in the middle of Ray's debate on local politics, but today I was watching a perfect example of island ingenuity.

It was 4:00 in the afternoon, close enough to quitting time that any die-hard Cruzan was off work and heading home. Each time a car pulled up for gas, the driver climbed out and tried to pump his gas. Once each customer discovered there was no gas pumping, he or she would walk into Ziggy's little store to explore why the pump was not pumping gas.

"Ziggy needs to put a sign on the pumps so people know he's out of gas," I said to myself as Mike, a local accountant, played with the pump for a few seconds and then marched into the gas station's convenience store. The answer came to me like a flash. Ziggy had not put a sign up that explained that he was "OUT OF GAS" on purpose. It dawned on me that Ziggy's failure to warn customers that he was out of gas was part of a master plan. It was critical to the "OUT OF GAS" master plan that gas customers entered the small store and discovered the wonders of his "ONE-DOLLAR" beer special. The pieces of the master plan began to fall into place. Ray, Cheri, and I had been the first victims of "Ziggy's master plan."

As I watched, the evil genius of Ziggy's "OUT OF GAS" master plan unfolded before me. Minutes after entering the small store to explore the mystery of no gas, Mike emerged with a one-dollar bottle of Elephant beer. I watched as he parked his ancient jeep next to my truck walked over to the little bar and sat down.

The detective in me was in full observation mode as gas customers began to fill the little makeshift bar. I watched in silence as each hapless victim of Ziggy's master plan forgot about gas and discovered cheap beer. Most of the gas customers were drawn like moths to the flame and joined us at the bar to fully exploit Ziggy's dollar beer special. I had an "I'll be damned moment" as I watched the "OUT OF GAS / ONE-DOLLAR" master plan unfolding into a full-blown party.

Ziggy's little open-air bar began to swell to capacity with the gasless. The boom box was turned up and Willie Nelson began howling about Whisky River. Mike began to hum to himself as the bartender retrieved his second beer. The bartender then left his duties for a few minutes, disappeared into the back of the building, and returned with a large stack of plastic chairs and, a stack of white plastic tables. To my amazement, the gasless began to pull the chairs and tables off the stacks and seat themselves. The master plan was about to bloom.

I told Ray to protect my coveted bar side seat and wandered behind the gas station to the men's and ladies' room. Ever the investigator, I peered into Ziggy's storage shed as I walked toward the restroom. The proof of Ziggy's plan was exposed. In the small dark plywood shed stood floor-to-ceiling stacks of white plastic chairs, little round side tables, and cases of cheap beer.

I smiled to myself, another plot exposed.

Like every great mastermind, Ziggy knew his market and had a plan, no gas, no worries, sell cheap beer!

My business finished, I returned to Ray and Cheri and eyed Ziggy's co-conspirator, the bearded bartender. He instantly placed another Elephant beer on the plywood bar in front of me. He smiled through his massive gray beard and said, "Ziggy got a hell of a deal on Elephant this week."

I raised the ice-cold beer in a toast and said, "Thank god for cheap beer." The smile reappeared through the gray mass of beard as the bartender handed beers to Cheri and Ray.

The clunk of the cold beer striking the wood of the bar brought my two associates out of their deep discussion and Ray said, "How much did Ziggy buy this stuff for?"

"Sixteen bucks a case at Plaza." The bartender said as he popped another beer and handed it to Ziggy's newest gasless customer.

"Wow," Cheri said.

Sixteen bucks a case for beer in St. Croix was an important fact in my growing understanding of Ziggy's master plan. I wondered how much Elephant beer a man could drink before the formaldehyde caused irreparable brain damage. The plot was thickening. I put the cold bottle to my parched lips and drank deeply.

Ray pulled out a five-dollar bill and pushed it across the bar. "Keep the change," he said.

"Nope," the bartender said as he pushed the five back." It's on Ziggy, but he asked if you guys could come back to the office and talk to him for a second".

"*Into the lion's den,*" I thought.

# CHAPTER 2

I have never been to the center of the Ziggy Empire, and as I stood at the brink of the doorway to his office, it took a second for my eyes to adjust to the dim lighting of the room. The room was a small cubical, I would guess it was no more than eight feet wide and ten feet deep. The room was lit by a single bare light bulb on the ceiling. The room seemed more like a closet than a room because each wall was lined from floor to ceiling with cases of Elephant and Pabst Blue Ribbon beer. I deduced that Pabst might be the next big one-dollar beer special.

Through the gloom at the end of the beer-lined corridor sat Mike Ziggler. He was sitting on a white plastic lawn chair, hunched over a small card table, his attention fixed on a laptop computer.

Sensing our presence, Ziggy stood up and turned toward me. "Hey, Mad Dog," he said as he began to move down the beer-lined corridor toward me.

"Hey, man," I replied offering my hand to Ziggy as he emerged from his office. Ziggy greeted us all and then led us back behind the building to a dilapidated wooden picnic table. "Have a seat," he said, and we all sat down.

"Thanks for the beer," Ray said as he raised his beer and took a long drink.

Cheri is not good at social foreplay but is a master at getting straight to the point. "What did you want to talk to us about?" she asked as she cautiously sat down at the ancient picnic table.

In response to Cheri's blunt question, Ziggy pulled a folded piece of newspaper out of his back pocket and opened it. For a second, he seemed to be studying the paper. Then he set it on the table's raw wood and smoothed the paper flat so we could all read the headline, " LOCAL MAN MISSING AND FEARED DROWNED."

"Terry Jeffery?" Ray said.

"Yep", Ziggy said with a slow nod.

"You want us to find him?" I asked.

"Nope," Ziggy said, and a dark look formed on his face, "he's dead."

"You know something the cops don't know?" Cheri asked, looking at Ziggy and then at me.

"Let me explain," Ziggy said as he slowly folded the article and put it back in his pocket.

"Terry and I are partners in a business called StreGo."

"StreGo?" I asked.

"Yeah, about a year ago, Steve Whistler, Terry, Sonny Rone, Sue Fox, and I all invested in a business called StreGo."

"How does the fact you were partners with Terry Jeffery give you insight into the fact he is dead instead of just missing?" Cheri asked.

"Simple," Ray said, giving Ziggy a dark look. "Steve Whistler and Sue Fox are both dead".

Ziggy's face paled, and he gave us a fearful smile. "Exactly," he said with a crack in his voice.

"Dead?" I asked, feeling like I had missed something.

"Dead." Ray repeated as he looked over at me, "You need to start reading the paper, Mad Dog. Steve Whistler was hit by a hit-and-run driver down on Queen Street about a week ago and Miss Fox was killed in her house up in Grape Tree estates."

"The police are investigating both deaths as possible homicides," Ziggy added.

"So, you think you're next?" I asked.

"Me or Sonny," Ziggy said.

"There is a little more to this," Ziggy explained, "We formed StreGo with six investors; a guy by the name of Charlie Thomas was also a partner. He had a heart attack about five months ago while he was working out at the gym. Charlie and Sue were the original people to come up with StreGo and came to the rest of us to invest.

"Charlie was the bodybuilder, wasn't he?" Cheri said.

"Yeah," Ziggy explained," he was getting ready to compete in the Mr. Universe competition when he had his heart attack."

"Yeah, I remember that," I said half to myself.

"So, what do you want from us?" Cheri asked, "We don't do protection work".

"Yeah, I know but you three do help people sometimes with investigations."

"Investigate exactly what?" I asked, but I didn't want anything to do with what should have been a major police investigation.

"Simple, Mad Dog, I want you guys to find out who is killing all my partners."

"And if we find out it's you?" Ray said, giving the gas station owner a long stare.

"I'll take that risk," Ziggy said with a smile.

"Three thousand a day plus expenses," Cheri said, to my surprise. The fee was outrageous, five times the normal fee if all three of us were working on a case together.

"Plus, a thirty thousand bonus if our work results in the conviction of anyone for the murder of any one of your partners, including you, and we work off a thirty-thousand-dollar retainer, and you put money in each time we make a draw, plus expenses," Ray said to my amazement. "Also, if we feel it is needed, we can bring in extra manpower and pay those persons out of the expense account. Finally, once every week you reimburse the account back to the original budget, so we know we have ample funding to do the investigation."

There was a long silence, and I wondered what insanity had come over Ray and Cheri. The fee they were talking about was astronomical. I gazed at them as they sat stone-faced, their eyes fixed on Ziggy.

"Done," Ziggy said, nodding his head.

I went numb; it was clear that Cheri and Ray had just been trying to bid the job so high that Ziggy would not use our services, but instead, Ziggy, not batting an eye, had trapped us into an agreement. If it had been a poker game, we would have just gone all in on a bluff, and Ziggy had just called our bluff without even a second of hesitation. I tried to show a positive face, but in truth, I knew we had just stepped into a very messy pile of shit.

Ziggy went all business and, without hesitation, said, "You will be working for StreGo, not me. StreGo's attorney is Martin Shields. I'll get ahold of Sonny and we will do a Corporate Resolution to hire and fund you by e-mail."

He paused and looked each of us in the eye. We nodded, and he continued, "Martin will draw up the paperwork, and I will ask him to fill you in on any specifics that may be important to your investigation. All of the funds that you will be paid will be from the corporation. I will instruct Martin to get your funds arranged so you can start work today. I know the police are already looking at Sonny and me as possible suspects, and I don't want that to interfere with your investigation, so please, no contact with me about the business end of our deal. Do everything through Martin. I will, of course, be available to meet with you three in the advancement of your investigation, but I ask that you please record all conversations we have."

Ziggy pulled two tape recorders out of the sweatshirt he was wearing. He then put one back in his pocket and pushed a second recorder toward us. "I have taken the liberty of recording this conversation," he said.

Then he pointed at the silver recorder on the table, "That's your recording of this conversation. I can't afford to have any questions about my actions in this matter. Please take the recorder and the recording of our meeting with you when you leave.

I felt a lump in my stomach begin to build and a throb in the back of my neck. It was over, we were hired. If we backed out now, we would be the black sheep phonies of the island.

Ziggy pulled a small tablet and a pen out of his pocket and did some figures. He then turned the small tablet around so the three of us could read what he had written down. "There will be seventy thousand dollars in the account. Thirty thousand will be earmarked as your retainer, which we will agree can be drawn on at any time; ten thousand will be earmarked as expenses, which again you can draw on at any time; and finally, thirty thousand will be earmarked as your bonus if your investigation results in the conviction of any person responsible for the killing of any of StreGo's partners. The bank will be instructed that the three of you are on the account so you can review the funds and draw funds from the account as needed."

"Who do we report to?" I asked.

"Martin will go over that with you, but as a layer of protection, Sonny and I agree that you are to take this investigation wherever it leads you. If it takes you to Sonny or my doorstep, pursue it no matter what."

Ziggy looked all three of us in the eye and then said in a calm voice, "We're done then?"

I sensed my last chance to stop the catastrophe. The negotiation had moved too fast but when I looked at Ray and Cheri, they gave me a small nod. "Done," I said, but for some reason, I felt the same sick feeling Alice must have felt stepping into the rabbit's hole.

"I will call Martin, and the three of you can meet with him in an hour at his office in Gallows' Bay; we can get the business part done. I will also instruct Martin to fill you in on StreGo and answer any questions you may have."

Ray stood, looked at Ziggy, and said, "Seems to me we got a little time till this meeting. How about three more ice-cold beers before we leave."

"That sounds fair. Let's drink a beer over our new business venture, and I sure hope you three figure this mess out quickly," Ziggy said.

Cheri picked the still-running tape recorder up off the table and clicked it off. The metal sound of the "click " was final. We were in the middle of a murder case just like that. Ray, Cheri, and Ziggy left the table and went back to the bar. I stood in the little office as a bad feeling washed over me.

I rubbed my bad shoulder and looked out over the green fields to the swirling sea. White foam was rising from the deep blue. Big, long swells were crashing huge waves across the island's outer reef.

In a voice only for my ears, I said, "Big waves, no wind, the calm before the storm," and the bad feeling turned into a chill that ran through me.

# CHAPTER 3

Lying in the dense brush overlooking Ziggy's gas station was a form of torture. The killer's elbows and knees ached from the hours of waiting. The dense spray of bug repellant was beginning to wear off, and the first of the biting ants were beginning to crawl over exposed flesh under the killer's camouflage suit. The Killer knew that soon the discomfort of the position would force a move away from the shooting position.

Wiping eyes to maintain a clear view of the target's gas station forced sweat to sting the tired eyes. After hours of lying in wait, the strong smell of a rotting animal in the dense bush still hung like a putrid fog over the killer's lair. Four hours on the hill, and the killer's patience was beginning to fray. The mark had appeared but only for a few seconds each time and never in a spot where a clear shot was possible.

Around four o'clock a white truck pulled up. The killer made a minor adjustment to the riflescope and brought the truck into clear focus. Ray Jones got out of the back seat of the truck. The killer knew Jones and his reputation. The big black man stretched like a lazy cat and eyed the area around the truck. "I'm right here you ass hole," the killer thought as Jones scanned the side of the hill where the killer hid. The killer wondered if Ziggy had hired him as a bodyguard. Jones was in his standard-issue black tee shirt and black jeans. The light flashed off the black wrap-around sunglasses that he wore. The killer imagined squeezing the trigger and watching Jones's chest explode. "Bang," the killer whispered and smiled.

The killer trained the high-powered scope on a man in jeans and a dark blue tee shirt who stood by the gas pump. "Out of gas, stupid," the killer thought as the man put down the gas nozzle and walked into the service station. Slowly the scope moved to the third rider in the truck, a woman that was now leaning against the truck talking to Jones. She was tall with long honey-colored hair. The faint hint of a bulge showed under her loose white blouse, a gun.

The man came out of the store and talked to his two partners.

The scope moved and followed Jones and the woman as they walked to the small bar at the side of the gas station.

After a moment, the killer remembered and whispered, "Mad Dog and Cheri Cotton," A new problem in the equation, or just three people going to Mike Ziggler's gas station for a beer, the killer wondered while gently stroking the rifle's trigger.

The killer wanted to pull away from the hill to move to somewhere comfortable but the three detectives had to be watched.

"Shit," the killer muttered as the three detectives left the bar and went into the back of the building. The killer now knew the truth. The disappearance of Terry Jeffery has caused the killer's next targets to hire protection. There was no escape for the merchant who called himself Ziggy. He was a dead man, and the three detectives could not protect him. The killer adjusted the scope of the assault rifle, bringing the little bar beside the gas station into close focus.

"If Ziggy comes out into the open, he will die, and the detectives can find another cash cow." The killer whispered with a feeling of power. In two hours, the light would be gone and the killer would have to leave the hiding place.

The first ant sting took the killer by surprise. The killer slowly set the rifle down, sat up, and inspected the bite.

Like the ant sting was an omen, the killer knew it was time to go and leave the hiding place for the day, but it was not time to quit the hunt. The killer thought about the three detectives and decided that following them could be productive. Carrying the day pack with food, water, ammo, and the rifle, the killer retreated through the thick brush.

Twenty minutes later, as the truck with the three detectives drove east toward Christiansted, the killer pulled out and followed the truck. As the truck turned into the area called Gallow's Bay, the killer said with a degree of self-satisfaction, "They're going to see Martin Shields's office." The detectives were now part of the game and the matrix of death. The killer smiled. The police had shown little interest, so the killer's mission had been just to kill, but now the game was moving to a new level. The three detectives would now test the killer's genius at administering death. The killer knew the reputation of the three detectives. In the last two years, they had brought down a major drug dealer and been responsible for the death of the East End serial killer who called himself PADDI.

These three were worthy opponents, and the game would now fully expose the killer's skill. The killer felt a flutter of excitement watching the big black man named Ray Jones and his two associates as they entered the lawyer's office.

With a smile, the killer pulled the two-page list of potential targets out of a backpack and inspected the list of names. Under the heading "TIER TWO" was "Martin Shields" and the figure 10%. Mr. Martin Shields was a worthy target. It was time to move to tier 2, and the lawyer would be first. Ziggy and Sonny Rone could wait. There were plenty of targets. Laying the list down, the killer thought, "I have all the time in the world."

# CHAPTER 4

I've known Martin Shields for years. He docks his sailboat four births down from where Cheri and I live on our boat, "Itchy Feet."

"You took the bait," he said with a smile as Ray, Cheri and I sat down across from him in his small conference room.

"Yep," Ray said with a deadpan look.

For some reason, Ray looked even more dangerous than usual as he folded his 6-foot 6-inch black-clad frame into Martin's brown leather conference chair. Sitting next to Ray, I was sure Martin was looking at his reflection in the black mirrors of Ray's sunglasses. Ray's attitude was dark and dangerous as he stared at Martin. The combination of being in a lawyer's office and signing a contract on a job he knew would be a headache was making Ray cranky. Ray is not a "contract" kind of a guy.

As I sat watching Martin and Ray as they had what could only be described as a stare-off, I wondered how deep a pile of shit we had landed in. The fact that Ziggy's little company was willing to pay a fee five times our normal costs was telling me it was a deep pile.

I finally decided to break the long silence between Ray and Martin." Do you have some contracts for us, Martin?"

Martin turned his attention away from Ray and opened a legal folder in front of him. Without a word he slid out four stapled documents and gave one to each of us, keeping the fourth.

Being pure business, he said to me, "You want an attorney to review this, Mad Dog."

"Let me take a look and then we'll decide."

With that, Martin stood up and walked to the conference room door. "I'll be outside when you're ready."

As the door closed behind the lawyer, Ray laid his hand on the contract and said, "Fuck me, man, I do not like this. The cops are going to freak if they think we're meddling in their ongoing murder investigations."

"By now, the first three are probably considered closed," I said.

"And what about Terry Jeffery? That sure as hell isn't closed," Cheri said in a near whisper, adding a shake of her head.

The whole deal had me worried, and I felt like I was trapped. I didn't like the case but didn't see a way to back out. "Are we going to do this or not?" I asked, unable to mask my concern.

"Shit," Ray said as he picked up the contract and began to read.

We all read until Cheri picked up a pen and signed her name. Without a word, she slid the signed contract over to me. I signed.

"Give me that," Ray said. I slid the paper to him, and he signed his name. All four copies had Martin Shields's name in blue ink above the title of StreGo Inc. Representative. "I think we sign all of these so each of us has a signed copy," I said. Cheri nodded, and we signed all the documents

I went to the door and opened it, and waved at Martin who was waiting on a couch just outside the door.

"Ready," I said.

Seconds later, Martin came into the conference room with his secretary, a small blond lady. He picked up one of the signed contracts, handed it to the secretary, and said, "Seven copies, please, Marty, and put this original in the StreGo file.

When the door closed behind his secretary, Martin sat down and said. "There are a few things you three need to know before you start."

"Let's start by why you think someone would kill three or maybe four people over some little piss ant company?" Cheri said, exposing the fact that she only wanted the facts.

In an almost protective gesture, Martin raised his hands and said, "Not piss ant, Cheri, not piss ant in any way. StreGo is already a huge company and getting bigger every day."

"Then, why is Ziggy still running his little gas station to make a living?" Cheri asked.

"It's complicated," Martin said as he sat back and his body language relaxed. He laced his fingers over his small beer belly, leaned back in his chair, and began talking. "Charlie Thomas and Sue Fox came to me about a year and a half ago wanting me to design a business model and corporate structure for a product they had designed."

Martin swiveled his chair around, opened a teak cabinet, and pulled out a round blue container about the size of a gallon jug. "This is "Strain 7," a revolutionary body-building protein designed by Charlie Thomas." The container was made of blue plastic with a dark blue screw-on lid. Martin unscrewed the top and exposed a white power. From where I was sitting, I could smell the overwhelming scent of warm milk.

Almost reverently, Martin screwed the top back on the large container and handed it to Ray.

"It's just a protein powder," Ray said more to himself than anyone at the table as he studied the label.

"Yeah, "Martin said, taking the container back, "Protein powder that sold over six million containers in the last eight months with a profit of over seventy-two million dollars."

The room went silent.

"Not piss ant," Cheri finally said in a small voice.

"I've never heard of it," I said

"Nope, not sold here anymore," Martin said, taking the container back and putting it back in the cabinet. "When Charlie and Sue came to me, they were selling the powder to bodybuilders at the various strength competitions that Charlie was competing in. They wanted to incorporate and have me build a business plan so they could distribute the product."

"At their request and based on Charlie's specific instructions, I structured a business model, a modified pyramid marketing scheme. The basic idea was to take the product to bodybuilding competitions and conventions and get the bodybuilders who chose to use Strain 7 to act as the marketers. There was one weird catch that Charlie insisted on."

"What" Cheri asked as she began to make notes on a legal pad sitting on the conference table.

"OK, I'll have to show you a diagram." Martin then pulled a rolled piece of white paper out and unrolled it.

At the bottom of the paper, I recognized six names in a line of boxes. They were the original owners of StreGo Ziggy had mentioned. Above the six boxes with the owner's names was a line of smaller boxes with dozens of names. The second row of boxes was labeled "TIER TWO OWNERS." A third line of boxes is labeled "TIER THREE OWNERS." This line consists of about one hundred boxes with names. Above the third tier of boxes, a large red arrow pointed up toward the top of the diagram. At the top of the paper, the words "NON-OWNER MARKETING MATRIX" were written.

"I put this together to explain the basic business model, and how it differs from normal pyramid marketing. He pointed at the bottom row. Ok, this tier of names, I will call the original owners of StreGo. They get a guaranteed ten percent of all StreGo profits, equally, shared between them. Here is one catch that is critical to your investigation. Under the corporate charter and bylaws, individual corporate ownership and profits in tier-one cannot be transferred by inheritance, sale, or gift by any original owner. What that means is: if one of the six first-tier owners dies, his percentage of the ten percent of profits from StreGo is allocated to surviving first-tier owners and will be divided by the surviving first-tier owners."

"Charlie dies and his profits go to the other five owners," I said, seeing the best reason for a murder I had ever witnessed.

"Exactly," Martin said.

"And there is a good chance that only two of the original six owners are still alive," Ray remarked as he took off his sunglasses and laid them on the table." So we only got 2 suspects, Ziggy and Sonny Rone."

"And, of course, Terry if he is still alive," I added.

"Not exactly," Martin said pointing at the second tier with about 25 names in a line of boxes. "If all six original owners were to die, the corporate structure allows the 10% owner's profits to go to the next tier.

Cheri's hand rose and she said, "Just a minute," and then began tapping on the calculator on her phone. "Let me get this straight. You mentioned seventy-two million dollars in profits, right?" She tapped on the phone calculator some more, "So 10 percent is about seven million dollars split between six that is now split between two owners."

"Correct," Martin said with a smile.

"But the second tier gets about 7 million between 25 of them and then if Ziggy and Sonny die and, of course, Terry is also dead, the whole bottom seven million is transferred from tier one to tier two shares, fourteen million between 25 people or about a half million apiece."

  "Why is Ziggy still driving a ten-year-old car then?" Ray said, giving everyone at the table a long stare.

"Simple," Martin said, pointing at the six boxes at the bottom, "The original owners agreed not to take their ten percent for the first year and to plow it back into the business to build a manufacturing plant in Puerto Rico. The plant was finished about 2 months ago, and the original owners are set to start taking monthly profits in about a month. Now, keep in mind this is a pyramid marketing plan, and it is growing at an exponential rate. Also, the no inheritance and no gift clause for the first-tier owners does not apply to the original owners' rights to the manufacturing plant that the six owners own free and clear."

"Also," Martin looked at all three of us, "Because Ziggy and Sonny now own the manufacturing plant, they have full product control. No one can mess with the business because the original owners own the only place where the product is manufactured. They have control of the product and, therefore, the money. When they withdrew their profits to build the plant, they added an ironclad control over the product's distribution."

What happens to the ownership of the manufacturing plant if everyone in tier one dies?" I asked.

Martin smiled and said, "Because it is a separate asset under a different business plan, it goes to the heirs of the tier-one owners.

"More suspects," Ray said.

"Some of the tier two and tier three members have tried to modify the distribution methods of the product but because the tier one owners control the flow of product, they hold the control of the marketing and product in an iron control."

"When the owners start taking profits, how much will they get?" I ask, trying to digest the size of the motive to kill.

"Sonny and Ziggy are set to receive checks around five hundred thousand dollars a month, which will build exponentially over the coming years, and if they both die, the people in the second tier will be getting Sonny and Ziggy's profits plus their own tier's profits which are significant. But there is a more important factor, the plant also realizes a profit of about two dollars a unit of the product."

"You guys will have other suspects to look at. Right now, the two living tier one owners own the plant, but if one dies, the other becomes the sole owner," Martin said.

"And, "Cheri added," that last survivor's heirs get the plant."

"Yep," Martin said, "but the plot thickens, second, and third-tier owners can sell their interest in the company, and a few tier-two and tier-three owners have sufficient funds to buy the manufacturing plant from any prospective heirs.

"And take full control?" Ray said.

"You got it.

"Who are the most likely suspects?" Cheri asked.

"Tom Severs, a Virgin Island's PD officer and a bodybuilder, controls almost 22 percent of the second tier. He got that large ownership percentage that he has built in two ways. First, he has a group of people he has brought into the third-tier of marketing, and second, he has purchased three of the other second-tier owner's percentages."

"Where is he getting the money to buy people out?" Cheri said as she moved over to stand above the diagram.

"Simple, the second-tier owners, unlike the original six owners, have been getting monthly checks. Six months ago, because Tom had such a strong group doing sales above him, he was getting checks over one hundred thousand dollars for months. He used his profits to buy some of the smaller second-tier owners out. Interestingly, one of the people who got out first was Charlie Taylor's mother Madge. She had a huge group of people in her marketing program and sold her whole interest to Tom for pennies on the dollar after Charlie died."

"Who else," I asked.

With a red pen, Martin put a red circle around Tom Sever's name and wrote 22 percent. He circled the name Ann Righter and wrote 15 percent, and Allen Bower wrote 15 percent.

"So those three own over 50 percent of tier-two?" Cheri said, writing down the names.

"Yep, they are the tier two owners who have been buying out owners. Remember in each tier because this is a pyramid marketing program, people are getting money from two sources. They own part of the company and get revenue from the upstream people they have brought into the organization. When Tom or Allen or one of the other more aggressive tier two owners buy out an owner, they don't just get the owner's piece of the ten percent profits, they get those owners upstream sales revenues too."

"Jesus," Ray said looking down on the marked paper that covered the conference table, "this is the land of the sharks. Little fish being eaten by big fish."

Martin smiled at Ray, "When Charlie told me what he wanted as far as a corporate structure, it was so weird, I asked him, why he was doing it this way. He said, I want my company to be survival of the fittest, I want it to work like nature."

"Lot a killing going on in nature," Ray said.

Cheri chuckled, and looked up at the three of us shaking her head, "This Charlie must have been a real piece of work."

I had to smile thinking of how warped the battle between owners would become as the huge profits rolled in. I laid my finger on the large group of names labeled tier three and said, "Any in tier three"

The lawyer smiled and circled one name "Antonio Mendoza." After circling the name, he wrote 38 percent next to the name.

"The Antonio Mendoza?" Ray said.

"The one and only," Martin said, "Mendoza has been very active in marketing Strain 7 and buying out anyone who wants to sell in tier three."

"I thought Mendoza got a 20-year sentence for running a Continuing Criminal Enterprise in the Federal Court," Cheri said.

"Sentence was reversed and the case dismissed," Martin said with a brief smile.

I made a mental note to take Antonio Mendoza to the top of our suspect list and then changed the subject. "That tier, the third tier, gets 10 percent of the profits?" I asked.

"Yeah, but after the third tier, the rest of the tiers are classic step marketing and not considered "owners" but are more like sales representatives paid a commission for their sales and the sales of people above them. Only the owners in the first three tiers will financially profit from the owner's deaths.

I looked at Cheri, who had finally quit taking notes, and reviewed the list of likely suspects. "How much of this do the VIPD investigators know?"

"Nothing, that's one of the reasons we decided to hire you guys. They don't even seem to care. I have tried to set up a meeting with the detectives in charge of the investigation and explain these motives and they won't even meet with me."

"We've got our work cut out for us," Cheri said as she looked up at Martin, "Where are we at with our fee?"

"I've put seventy thousand dollars in this account," Martin said as he slid a checkbook across the table. You're expected across the street at the bank to sign signature cards. I will deposit funds weekly to keep the balance at seventy thousand dollars."

I looked at the checkbook and said to Martin, "Only one more thing. You mentioned that Strain 7 is not sold in St. Croix. Why not?"

"Strain 7 has a group of growth steroids in its ingredients that make it illegal to sell in the United States. All of our customers are international."

"But they make it in Puerto Rico." I clarified.

"Yep, welcome to the good old U. S. of A. We can't sell in the United States, but a loophole in the law lets us manufacture."

"And one more thing," Ray said, looking into Martin's eyes with a hawk-like glare, "you own a share in tier two?"

"Yes, I own 10% of tier two. I traded it with the original owners for my legal fee. I have never helped to market StreGo so I am not part of the pyramid program

"So, if Ziggy and Sonny get killed, you will double your income because the tier-one funds will then be added to the tier-two funds," Ray said.

"Yep," Martin said.

"How much did you get last month?" I asked trying to wrap my mind around the money part of the motive to kill.

"Forty-two thousand dollars," Martin said again without emotion.

"Just for fun, Martin," Cheri asked, sitting back in her chair, "Can I give you a hypothetical, Sonny and Ziggy go to the big bank in the sky tomorrow. What will your check be next month?"

Martin thought for a second before he spoke, "About ninety thousand If all the tier-one members die." He rolled up the chart and handed it to me. "I know we're talking about a lot of money, Mad Dog, but believe me, I don't want to die, and I think we're all at risk. If the crazy bastard that is doing this will kill four people to make more money, why not kill us all?"

# CHAPTER 5

The sun was moving toward the horizon when the three detectives emerged from the lawyer's office and walked across the open parking lot to the Bank of St. Croix.

The killer, having pulled off the camouflage clothing worn during the afternoon surveillance, exited the car and walked casually to the lawyer's office. As the killer opened the door to Martin Shields's office, Marty Taylor rose to greet the potential client. Without hesitation, the killer raised a silenced twenty-two caliber pistol and shot Marty Taylor in the forehead, killing her instantly.

"Sorry," the killer said as the small woman crumpled to the ground.

Without hesitation, the killer proceeded to the office of Martin Shields Esquire, opened the door, and from the doorway, shot the lawyer in the forehead.

# CHAPTER 6

I was in a deep sleep when our cell phone rang. As Cheri groped for the phone, I looked up at the three bright blurs of the digital clock on the dresser across from our bed. Ignoring Cheri's scramble for the phone, I stared until the three blurs of light transformed into "4:30." "What the fuck is someone calling us at four thirty," I growled, the jolt of being woken from a dead sleep was quickly transforming into a sour mood.

"Shushh," Cheri said as she pulled the phone to her ear. "Hello," she said.

After a long silence, she said, "You gotta be shitting me."

The light flicked on, and I mouthed, "What?"

Cheri shook her head and raised her finger, gesturing to "give her a minute."

"When?" she said as she got up and pulled her robe from the hook on the wall.

There was a long silence and then she said, "Come to the boat and I'll have coffee ready," a pause, and then she said, "Yeah, fifteen is good," and hung up.

"Well," I said.

"Get dressed, we got a little problem," she said as she stepped over to the steps and started up the stairs to the salon.

"What's up?"

Cheri stopped halfway up the steps and turned to me. I could see a combination of pain and anger in her hard look. "Some son of a bitch killed Martin and his secretary last night." She said her voice flat.

"Martin Shields?" I asked.

"Yeah," she said as she turned and finished climbing into the salon. "That was Ray. He'll be here in a few minutes, so I need to brew some coffee, and you need to get dressed."

The coffee pot had just finished filling when I felt Ray climb on the back deck of our boat and heard him coming around to the port salon hatchway.

I poured coffee into the three cups Cheri had laid out before she went to the stateroom to dress. I handed Ray his cup as he came into our galley. I wasn't in the mood to be polite, so I asked, "What do you know?" as Ray took his cup of coffee.

"Where's Cheri?" he asked.

"Below getting dressed."

"Let's wait," he said, sagging into one of the recliners that line the port side of our salon, "I don't want to tell this story twice."

I went into the forward berth, got a folding chair we keep for guests, and sat down in it, leaving the other recliner for Cheri.

While we waited, I tried to gather my still sleepy mind, and Ray sat back in the recliner and sipped his coffee.

In less than a minute, Cheri came out of our stateroom. She had on levies and her Wyoming Cowboys sweatshirt. Under the sweatshirt, I saw the faint bulge of her Glock 40 pistol.

She walked to the counter, took her blue thermos cup, and turned to Ray.

"Ok, Jones, I guess we need to know what's going on."

Ray gestured toward the empty recliner, and Cheri moved over and sat.

Ray first centered on me and then moved his gaze to Cheri. "OK, about 20 minutes ago an old buddy at the PD called me and said that Martin's girlfriend found Martin and his secretary shot to death in his office."

"When?" I asked

"My contact said that Martin's girlfriend had a date with him at six thirty and when he didn't show, she went to his office and found him. Then she called the police, who have been there all night, working the scene." Ray paused for a second and then said. "My source said the cops found our contract with StreGo on Martin's desk. He thinks we'll get a call to come in and make a statement this morning and wanted to give me a heads up."

"Why talk to us?" Cheri asked.

Ray shrugged,

"Simple," I said. "Martin keeps that tablet at his desk, that he marks his time down on. The cops probably looked at the tablet and the contract and figured out we saw Martin just before his death.

Ray nodded. "Makes sense."

"I'm not huge on letting VIPD know we're working three of their active homicides and a missing person," Cheri said as she got up and began building a second pot of coffee.

When we agreed to take the StreGo case, our primary concern was the possibility of causing bad blood with the homicide detectives because we were working on an active case. With Martin and Marty's homicide, we were now smack dab in the middle of the VIPD investigation. The StreGo case had gone from bad to nightmare, and all we had done was get a little sleep.

"Fuck it, we just don't tell the cops what the contract is for. We tell them we have a client, and his business is confidential." Ray said finishing his coffee and holding the cup toward Cheri like his need for coffee would make the old black coffee maker perk faster.

"There's a plan, Jones, that should keep us out of the shitter for about a minute and a half till they go talk to Ziggy, whose name is also on the contract," Cheri said, pulling the half-full pot out of the maker and pouring Ray his second cup.

"Cheri is right. If they pull us in for an interview, we need to be straight with them."

"We do have a duty of confidentiality," Cheri said.

"You need to make up your mind," I replied as I put my big red mug out for a refill.

"All this what's right what's wrong bullshit is why I hate this job," Ray said standing up and seeming to fill our small salon with menace. "How about we turn off our phones, get out on the street, and start working this case? The odds are the cops will be plenty busy and completely forget about talking to us if they can't get ahold of us in the next couple of days."

"Out of sight out of mind," I said.

"Out of sight out of mind," Cheri said.

Ray smiled.

Sometimes the simplest answer is the best answer, and sometimes the simplest answer is the dumbest thing you could do.

# CHAPTER 7

We split up, and based on the information Martin and Ziggy had given me, I met with the first investors at Beaston Hill's gym at seven o'clock that morning. Tony Morgan and Abe Carter explained they were early investors and admitted that one of the early advantages of being an investor was that Charlie Thomas and, after his death, Steve Whistler had made sure that investors would still get a steady supply of StreGo powder.

"What the hell, man," Morgan said between grunts as he pushed a pair of steel disks that looked like they came off the front wheels of a locomotive up into the air with his legs. "If I want to strive for the perfect body and StreGo helps, who are they to say no."

I agreed, and Morgan smiled. I know how to win friends and influence people.

"Yeah," Mr. Carter, a five-foot-six-inch box of muscle agreed as he hoisted dumbbells that resembled engine blocks.

I wondered if either of these steroid millionaires would survive the investor bloodbath that seemed to be taking place.

"Either of you guys heard from the cops?" I asked.

"Like they came and talked to us or something?" Carter asked between grunts.

"Yup."

"Why would cops want to talk to us?" Morgan asked.

"Because you knew a bunch of the murder victims," I said, trying to get back on track.

"Like who?" Mr. Carter, he asked.

"Like Charlie Thomas and Steve Whistler."

The two musclemen looked at each other, and both set down their iron burdens.

"Man, what are you talking about, Charlie had a heart attack in this gym right over there," Carter said as he pointed to a corner where a set of weights rested.

"Yeah, and Steve got whacked by a drunk driver," Morgan added

"How about Terry Jeffery and Sue Fox?" I asked.

"Who?" They replied in perfect unison.

"You don't know them?" I asked.

"Nope," they said again in perfect unison. I was starting to wonder if steroid abuse could cause mind melds.

"Do you understand the marketing and corporate structure of StreGo?" I asked.

"Like it's some kind of pyramid thing," Morgan said, pulling a dirty white towel over his shoulder.

"Yeah, we invest, and they send us money and if we get other guys to invest, we get more money. Sure, we understand. We must, right, we get a check once a month." Carter said just like he understood the whole program.

Running on a hunch, I asked, "Who would benefit from, say, Steve Whistler dying?"

Back to one brain, they both shrugged.

"Do you know what a tier is in StreGo?"

One brain but only gap-jawed confusion.

"So, you don't know you're tier two investors?" I asked.

"What?" Carter asked.

"How much do you get a month from StreGo?" I asked

"Don't know," Carter said with a shrug, "After my third check, I quit work, and I just haven't looked lately. My old lady does all the bookkeeping."

I looked at Morgan but only got a shrug.

"Tony and I quit work so we could build full-time. Our wives run the houses, and we lift." Carter said as if the statement was an explanation.

"But you invested money in StreGo?"

"Damn right," Morgan said, "Charlie said if we invested, he could keep us in StreGo even though the bullshit feds wouldn't allow it to be sold here on the island."

"Yep," from Carter.

"Do you get more or less money now," I asked trying to gauge how clueless these two were.

Back to one brain, they looked at each other and shrugged.

"Thanks for the chat, guys," I said as I stood. Carter smiled and said, "Hey, Mad Dog, you ought to get in here and lift once in a while. It will get rid of some of that flab."

One brain, they both smiled.

"Yeah," I said, tapping my belly with both hands, "a little iron could firm me right up."

One brain, same smiles.

"Take care, guys."

On the way out, a pretty twenty-something blond in a sleeveless shirt yelled from behind the counter, "Hey, Mad Dog, how's it going?"

"Randy," I said and came over to the counter. "I thought you were working at the Thai Restaurant."

"Second job," Randy bubbled, "and I get free membership."

"Cool," I said basically because I was short on words after my last little sit-down with the muscle twins.

"You and the Lady Cotton should join. I could give you a great deal this week."

"No thanks, but maybe you could help me," I said.

"Sure, what you need?" she said, bursting with enthusiasm. Where does all that joy come from?

"First, the two guys upstairs, Mr. Morgan and Mr. Carter. Can you tell me anything about them?"

"Sure," she said, moving forward and dropping her voice. Those two are way serious but a little slow. " She paused and then said, "You know?"

"Noticed."

She beamed a toothpaste commercial smile. "They're here every day from seven in the morning until two in the afternoon and then back at it at five and workout until eight or nine in the evening."

"Last night," I asked.

"Yep, the restaurant closes on Monday, so Mike gives me a late shift. Those two guys were the last to leave last night. Kinda aggravates me, we're supposed to close at eight, but every Monday I'm late getting home because they take their time."

"Bummer," I said, wondering where that slip into the 70s had come from.

"Oh well," she said with a smile and a shrug, "don't punch the old timecard till the last soul is gone, so the extra cash only helps."

"Yep," I said and waved goodbye. "Two down and 30 to go," I muttered as I walked out the door.

# CHAPTER 8

By noon, I had managed three more interviews that were all dead ends and headed downtown to Harvey's for lunch with Cheri and Ray. When I walked into our favorite Ma and Pa diner, Ray and Cheri were waiting. Ray had already finished half a beer, and Cheri was drinking a bottled water.

"Ordered the skirt steak for you," Ray said as I sat down.

Cheri said. "I found out that two of the men on my list were working and had solid alibis for last night when Martin was killed. Also, Max Ortiz was in Puerto Rico when Whistler got run down and when Sue Fox was killed."

"I met the bodybuilders, Mr. Carter and Mr. Morgan, who are off the list. I also crossed off these three." I showed Cheri my list.

"How about you?" Cheri asked Ray.

Ray smiled and said, "Streets are silent, but the word is floating."

"How many beers has he had?" I asked Cheri.

"Streets are silent, but the word is floating?" Cheri said, looking at Ray, who was waving at the waitress for a refill on his Heineken. "Should I quote you in our report to Ziggy or just paraphrase?"

 "Whatever makes sense," was all Ray said as he got up and went to the restroom in the back of the restaurant.

I looked at Cheri and asked, "What's with Ray?"

She smiled and pulled out the interview list we had made using the information we had gotten from Ziggy and Martin. She pointed at Cindy Childers, a name on the list.

"Ok," I said, reading the name, "Who's Cindy Childers?"

"Cindy used to work for Scotia Bank before she hit the jackpot with StreGo."

I thought for a second and then remembered. "The tall lady always worked in loans."

"That's her," Cheri said with another knowing smile.

"So, Ray had to interview his old flame today?"

"Yeah, and now she's another potential StreGo millionaire."

"You think he's going to try to rekindle the old flame," I asked, remembering the nightmare three years earlier that had been Ray's fling with Cindy Childers. Cindy was a beautiful and headstrong woman and, in their brief relationship, had raised Ray into the thin-air strata of love and then down into the pits of hell. Cheri and I could laugh about Ray's behavior during his fling with Cindy now, but being Ray's friend had been an ordeal during his relationship with Cindy.

"This is the worst day of my life," Cheri said with a smile.

I smiled at the memory of Ray walking on the boat about once a week, saying, "This is the worst day of my life," and then relaying the most recent battle with Cindy. "She's not good news," I said.

"Kryptonite," Cheri said with a smile as we watched Ray return to the table.

"So, you met with Cindy today?" I said as Ray walked up to the table.

"Forgot how fine that woman was," Ray said with a faraway smile.

"Find anything out?" I asked, trying to keep things business.

Ray turned to me and nodded, "The lady still has the fire," he said.

"Anything about our case, you know, StreGo, the thousand dollars a day you get?"

"Nope, just that she quit her job and has money flowing into her account faster than she can spend it."

"Anything else," I asked.

"Nope, we didn't talk much."

"Interview anyone else on your list?" I asked.

"Nope, ran out of time."

"Rich, smart, and beautiful," Cheri said, giving a playful smile, "We're not going to have to live through another summer of Cindy versus Ray, are we?"

"No way," Ray said, straightening up and turning his black shades toward Cheri. "We're more mature now. We're taking it slow. A little dinner tonight and, you know, take it slow. None of that crazy shit this time. I mean, you know."

We nodded in agreement, and Ray was saved from any more questions as the waitress showed up with three heaping plates of food. The rich aroma of seared meat and stewed greens rose from the plates as she set our meals down. I ordered a Diet Coke and dove into the sizzling skirt steak.

"I ran into one little issue today," I said between bites. It seems Charlie Taylor was supplying investors with StreGo."

"That's just a fancy way to say he was dealing steroids; this is turning into my kind of case," Ray said, taking a swig of his beer.

"That adds another layer of motives, but Taylor is dead now," Cheri said.

"Yeah," I agreed, "but Steve Whistler took over supplying the steroid, according to the muscle men at the gym."

"With Whistler dead, who's supplying the steroids now?" Cheri asked.

I gave myself a mental kick, "I didn't ask," I said.

"Probably need to know that," Ray said, "maybe Ziggy knows."

"I'll put it on my list to call and ask," I said.

"Another interesting twist," Cheri said, "none of my people knew their interest in StreGo was passed to the partners. It's in the fine print of the investor agreements, but none of the people I talked to seemed to understand that part of the agreement, or at least they said they didn't." Cheri said.

"Cindy understood it and is scared to death. She said killing Martin means the killer is moving into the second tier," Ray said and then smiled. "I told her I'd protect her and have her hid out at my crib for the time being."

Cheri and I glanced at each other, and Cheri said, "Big responsibility, Ray."

"Yep," Ray said.

"So, Cindy is at your place now?" I asked.

"Yep, gonna get some of this fine skirt steak and take it home to her as soon as we're done."

"How are you going to work the case," I asked, "if you're guarding Cindy?"

Ray seemed to pause and then said. "It'll all work out."

I sipped on the Diet Coke the waitress had brought over and considered the last eighteen hours. In just eighteen hours, our case had ballooned into a hurricane-grade nightmare, taking every conceivable bad turn. Bad enough at the start with us investigating a possible four active homicides, but now two more homicides and we were dodging the cops, even though we were arguably the last three people to see Martin and his secretary before their murder. Now it was clear that the victims were actively dealing illegal steroids to investors and, to top off the list, Ray was in a love plunge with Madam Kryptonite and now had her holed up at his house. I thought to myself, how could this get any worse when the door to Harvey's swung open and Dory Hancock rolled his five foot ten, two-hundred-and-eighty-pound body through Harvey's front door. Dory is a bald black man with big piercing eyes, and those eyes were locked on our table like a hawk spotting a lizard.

"Afternoon," he said in his deep voice, "I have been looking for you three, you got a minute?"

I motioned toward the fourth seat, and Cheri moved her backpack so Dory could sit down.

"How could we help you, Lieutenant?" I asked in my most innocent voice.

"You know that Attorney Shields and his secretary, Miss Andrea Chambers, were shot and killed at Attorney Shields' office last night?"

"We were just discussing that, Lieutenant," Cheri said, putting on her best-shocked face, "as a matter of fact, we were at Mr. Shields' office around four in the afternoon to sign some contracts."

Hancock flipped open his notebook and said, "Yes, a retainer agreement with a company called StreGo, as I understand it."

"Yep," Ray said.

"Mind telling me when you left and where you were until six that evening?"

Cheri answered, "Well, the contract we signed with StreGo involved some initial payments, so we went across the street to the bank to withdraw the advance funds. Then, Mad Dog and I went back to our boat, and I suspect Ray went home."

"No home for me. I went to Cheeseburgers for a beer," Ray said with a smile.

"Thanks," Hancock said and rose. "Any idea exactly what time you left Attorney Shields' office."

"Let me look," Cheri said, and she pulled the receipt out of her purse for the bank, "according to this receipt, we got the money from the bank at 4:47. My best guess is that we left Martin's office at about 4:40."

"Other than business, were you acquainted with Attorney Shields or Miss Chambers?"

"Martin was a good friend. He kept his boat just down from ours at the marina, and Ray did a lot of work on it. So, I'd say Martin was a good friend to all three of us."

"Ditto," Ray added, "Martin was a good man. This is a bad day."

Hancock said, "Sorry for your loss. I want you to know I'll do everything I can to find and prosecute the person who did this. Attorney Shields and Miss Chambers will both be missed," the homicide detective sounded sincere, but his eyes spent an extra second on Ray, and I wondered what he was really thinking.

"Did you notice anything odd at Attorney Shields' office or in the parking lot?"

"Nope," Ray said.

Both Cheri and I gave the detective a headshake.

"Well, that's about it for now, but I may need to talk to you later. Is that OK?"

We all assured the detective he could call us any time, and he stood up to leave. He walked about two steps toward the door and then turned to Cheri. "Mrs. Cotton, may I have that receipt as evidence? It may help us define the time of death."

"Of course," Cheri said as she reached into her purse and handed the detective the bank receipt.

"Thank you," the detective said. He gave us a small smile and left, waving at Harvey as he went out the door.

Cheri nodded, and we returned to our cooling steaks.

"Well, we dodged that bullet," Ray said, watching the door Detective Hancock had left by.

As I chewed my lukewarm skirt steak, I thought. Two more people dead, misleading, if not lying, to a homicide detective in a homicide investigation, Ray twisted by lust slash love, the victims actively distributing illegal steroids and a set of motives and suspects that were reproducing like roaches on fertility drugs. The simple fact was that the three thousand dollar-a-day retainer was already starting to look like a discount.

# CHAPTER 9

After lunch, we split up again. Ray drove back to Cindy Childers's house to "protect her," and Cheri and I went to meet Charlie Thomas's mother, Madge Thomas. Madge Thomas lived in a small yellow house in Estate Peter's Rest.

The house had a large fenced yard, and the east side of Madge Thomas's yard was covered with a large garden that was ready to harvest. From the road, I could see the red of ripe tomatoes dotting a long row of well-kept tomato plants. Around the taller green bushes of tomatoes were neat lines of lettuce and other greens. Toward the back of the lot were two large mango trees and a huge breadfruit tree whose limbs towered over the entire back half of the property.

In the back of the garden, on her hands and knees, a stout black woman wearing bright orange pants and a flowered shirt. On her head was a sombrero that was bright pink.

"Wonder if she's selling her tomatoes," Cheri said as we sat in the truck looking over the property.

"We'll have to ask," I said. Cheri loves fresh vegetables and never misses a chance to stock up.

Cheri looked at the list of interviews and said, "Look, I think it's important we both talk to Charlie's mom. She seems to be a wealth of historical information on StreGo, but after we meet with her, I should take you back to the car, and we should split up and hit as many investors as we can."

"That works," I said as we climbed out of the truck.

When I came around the truck, Cheri was already standing at the fence waving at the lady gardener in the hot pink sombrero. "You Ho!" she shouted, waving her right hand until the sombrero rose and the gardener waved.

"Hi," Cheri shouted, "Are you Madge?"

The woman rose to her full height and walked toward us without speaking. As she approached us, she slowly pulled flowered gardening gloves off her hands and smacked them against her thigh to knock off the deep brown dirt covering them.

"Hi," Cheri said again as the woman approached us, "Are you Madge Thomas?"

"I am, honey," the woman said in a deep, heavily accented southern drawl.

"Hi, I'm Cheri Cotton," Cheri said, "and this is my husband... ."

"Yes," the woman said, interrupting Cheri mid-sentence, "The famous or should I say infamous Mad Dog Cotton," offering her hand to Cheri but looking me straight in the eye.

Madge Thomas was a big woman but not fat. She was powerful in a hard-working way. She stood a full six feet tall, and in her loud, flowered clothes and bright pink hat, she seemed almost intimidating. She fixed her relaxed gaze on me and stretched the word "infamous" into about four long syllables. I smiled, but a response got caught in my throat.

After shaking Cheri's hand, she offered her hand to me. Her hand was hard with calluses, and I could feel the power of real strength as we shook hands, but Madge Thomas's handshake was gentle. She gently held my hand, not moving, for a moment, and stared into my eyes.

"You're here about my son," she said, still grasping my hand. Her soft brown eyes seemed to be trying to bore into my thoughts. "Here to ask me about my poor boy Charlie."

I wanted to pull my hand away to move back a small step. The big woman's presence seemed overwhelming, like meeting a charismatic preacher or politician. The combination of her soft southern voice, her fixed penetrating gaze, and the gentle but strong hold she had on my hand created a strange intimacy that left me slightly uncomfortable

Cheri came to my rescue and said, "Mad Dog and I did want to talk briefly about StreGo and your son's involvement in the company if we could."

Slowly, Mrs. Thomas turned her eyes to Cheri, and a small smile crossed her face, "Of course, dear," she said and finally released my hand. "Please, come into the backyard, and we can have a nice glass of tea and talk."

When Cheri spoke, and Madge Thomas's hand and eyes released me, it was almost like being released from some unseen power. I had to blink and regroup a little.

While I stood trying to get a handle on what had just happened, Cheri and Mrs. Thomas moved down the fence to the gate directly in front of the small yellow house. Without comment, I followed Cheri and Mrs. Thomas into the backyard. Behind the house was a small sitting area with a picnic table on a small raised cement patio. The sitting area was cool under the protective leaves of a massive breadfruit tree, and around the raised patio was a flower garden that created an atmosphere rich with the smells of blooming flowers and a rainbow of colors created by hundreds of roses and orchids. Nearly hidden in the nest of flowers was a large yellow cat. The cat sat silently alert, ears forward, watching us intently.

"Please sit," Mrs. Thomas said. With an exaggerated movement of her hand, she directed us to the bench on the side of the picnic table facing the house.

After we were seated, she sat facing us and fixed me again with a long gaze. "So, Mr. Cotton," she said, ignoring Cheri, "How can I help you?"

# CHAPTER 10

My normal practice is to let Cheri lead interviews so I can sit and observe the person we're talking to, but Madge Thomas had taken control of this interview, and I was forced to lead off.

"Well", I said, "Mrs. Thomas...."

She raised her big hand, and I stopped in mid-sentence, "Please, Mad Dog, no one has called me Mrs. Thomas since I taught school, call me Madge."

I took a second to regroup, noticing a quick smile from Cheri.

"Well," I began again, "Cheri and I were hoping you could help us with some background understanding of your son's company, StreGo."

"I see," she said, her eyes still fixed on me and ignoring Cheri.

There was a long silence while I waited for her to continue, but she only gazed at me.

Finally, I said, "Is that ok?"

"Yes," she said, "of course, I suspect this may have to do with the deaths of so many of Charlie's associates."

Madge's constant eye contact was beginning to cause the same uncomfortable feeling I had felt at the fence, and I turned to Cheri. Cheri gave me a hint of a smile but said nothing.

I looked back at Madge and said in a business voice I never use. "StreGo has retained us to look into the deaths of certain people who were associated with your son's company." I hate people who talk in Mr. Business, tone like I had just done. Deep in the forest of my mind, I winched at how I must have sounded.

My business tongue only earned me another smile from Madge Thomas. Again, the world of sweet smells and bright colors on the small patio went silent. The yellow cat's dark eyes glowed from beneath a hallow of red and yellow flowers. I took a quick breath and continued.

"We were told that at the beginning of StreGo, you were very active in developing your son's company."

"Yes," she said, drawing the word out in slow, long syllables that made the words seem more a question than a statement.

"Can you tell me anything that may help me understand the deaths of your son's partners?"

Madge sat back slightly, and to my relief, she turned her gaze to Cheri and pulled the large hat from her head, setting it beside her on the bench.

"Well, Mad Dog, I suspect they are killing each other off because of the no inheritance clause in the partnership agreement and the large amount of money involved." Her statement, and the matter of fact, way she had said it, left me silent, one more time.

"Explain," Cheri said, coming to my rescue.

"Well, I'm sure Mr. Ziggler has explained to you that the fine print in the partnership agreements for the first three tiers of StreGo passes the ownership of any interest on to the surviving partners upon the death of any partner."

"Yes," Cheri said, taking the interview over.

"As I understand it, StreGo has ballooned into a very lucrative business since Charlie died, and I would not be surprised if one or more of his partners or associates are killing off the rest of the group to enlarge their share of the company."

"Do you still have an interest in StreGo?" Cheri asked.

The soft gentleness of Madge Thompson's face hardened. "No," she said, any hint of the gentle southern accent gone.

"I understand you were a first-tier owner at one time." Cheri said, "First-tier owners are in line for millions now."

"I sold all of my interest in Charles's company after he was killed." She said flatly.

"We spoke to Mr. Shields, Charlie's attorney, and he said that your son specifically requested the small print that moved ownership to surviving partners." I said, "Do you know why he made that request?"

She shifted her gaze back to me directly, and the hardness left her face, replaced by calm gentleness. "Charles believed, as I do, that assets gained without effort are evil and that only people who work to build an asset should benefit from it. The Lord put us on this earth to labor, Mad Dog, and be the best person we can be within his plan. When a person benefits from another's toil, it weakens them and goes against them becoming the best they can be within god's plan."

"So," Cheri said. "Charlie does not believe in inheritance?"

"Correct," she said, briefly looking at Cheri before bringing her brown-eyed gaze to me.

"Makes sense," I said.

She nodded like a second-grade teacher who had just witnessed a student grasp a new idea. "Charlie worked hard to perfect his business, and his associates gave him money that allowed his vision to grow."

"Why did you sell out of StreGo?" I asked, "Didn't you believe in the company anymore?"

Small pools of liquid gathered at the bottom of Madge Thomas's eyes, and she said in a small voice. "When Charles was gone, the money and the ownership of the company had no soul for me. I knew I had to get away from the business. I loved the business and Charlie's idea. When I watched it grow, and Charlie cared for it like I tend to my garden, I was proud. But after he died, the whole thing seemed dark and uncaring, and I had to get away from it."

I didn't understand the words, but I understood the emotion. I said, "I understand."

She nodded and, with her hand, wiped the pools of liquid from her eyes.

I sensed that it was time to leave. We had more to learn, but for some reason, I looked at Cheri, and she gave me a small smile and nod that said, "Let's go."

"Madge, thanks for the time you gave us. Can we come back and talk some other time?" I asked.

'Of course, Mad Dog," she said, her soft southern drawl in full bloom. "Can you find your way out? Your questions have stirred my heart up, and I want to sit here with Charlie."

We both stood up, and Cheri gave Madge's hand a small pat.

As we walked out of the blanket of shade that was created by the giant breadfruit tree, Cheri said, "That was weird,"

# CHAPTER 11

Ziggy gave me a big smile as I described our interview with Madge Thomas. "Yep, he said that is one seriously different human being. I used to meet with Charlie, and she would be there. I bet I ran into her at the office thirty times, and she never once said hello."

Cheri bumped my arm and said in a half-joking way. "Well, old Mad Dog had her eating out of his hands. You would have thought the old gal was head over heels in love with him. She couldn't even take her eyes off him."

I smiled and shrugged.

Ziggy shook his head and smiled, "Well, Mad Dog, good luck with that one. Did she tell you anything important to find out what's going on?"

"Nope," I said, "but she did explain why Charlie set the company up so all the ownership of a deceased partner passes to the partners and not the heirs of the deceased."

"Really, "Ziggy scooted up in his chair and leaned forward, "I always wondered what the hell he was thinking."

"In a nutshell, he and his mom believe that you should only get what you earn, and inheritance is a bad thing," Cheri said, sipping her free dark rum and diet coke.

"Seems to me that brilliant idea backfired," Ziggy said.

"Yep," I said, "Even though the profits seem to be skyrocketing, I don't think you could give me any stock in StreGo right now."

"I wish I could give you mine right now and just run my little business in peace." He said, taking a long sip of his Elephant beer, "I feel like I got a target on my head, and I'm afraid to even drive home."

# CHAPTER 12

The killer smiled at the target and two of his detectives just sitting there waiting to be killed. The killer knew that killing the detectives at this point would be a mistake. They were making the game finally interesting.

The man who called himself Mad Dog seemed confused and often just fumbling forward, but the killer knew differently. The killer watched the man, and he knew a dangerous opponent when he saw one. The other detective, Jones, was dangerous, but he was predictable, and now that he was watching the woman, she would not be a problem. The killer smiled at the thought of killing them both together and the pain that would cause Mad Dog and his wife.

The bearded bartender picked up a bottle of tequila and began pouring a shot for the target. It was time to let the detectives know they could not protect the target. No one could.

The high-powered rifle barked once, and the killer began to melt back into the bush.

# CHAPTER 13

I sensed the tequila bottle explode before my brain registered the gunshot. Cheri was moving for the floor before I could react, so I grabbed Ziggy and threw him to the floor. I kicked the heavy table beside us over to make cover and began following Cheri, who was crawling for cover beside the heavy plywood bar. Ziggy and two other patrons were right behind me. We all were forced to crawl through the fragments of the shattered bottle as we rounded the bar and scooted on all fours behind the cinder block of the building.

I had small cuts on both my hands and my right knee when I finally reached the cover of the building and stood up. Ted, the bartender, had turned and went through the door and into the gas station's small kitchen when the bottle had exploded. As I looked around, I could see blood splatter across the back of the bar. "Ted," I yelled around the corner, "You, OK?"

From inside came an angry growl, "I'm just fucking fine. That fucking bottle cut the shit out of my hand."

"Anybody hit?" Cheri asked. Her Glock 40 was out, but the fire in her eyes looked more dangerous than the black pistol.

"We're all fine," an older man said, "just some cuts from crawling around on the ground."

"Where?' I asked Cheri

"The hill, I think."

Her answer confirmed my impression that the shot had come from the hill. I looked at the brown wooden wall to my left and saw what looked like a bullet strike on the wood. I mentally calculated the angle from the tequila bottle to the wall. "Hill about mid-way up," I said as I stepped around the corner and leveled my pistol on the hill where I thought the shot had come from.

Cheri followed me, and we moved behind the open-air bar and down to the end, where the sidebar protected us. I scanned the bush for any movement but saw none.

"Shit," Cheri said. "I don't see anything."

"Me either," Ziggy said from behind her.

"Got damn it, Ziggler, get your ass back behind the building." I snapped.

I could hear him scooting back.

"I want to pop a couple of caps on the hill," I said, the adrenaline still rushing through me.

"Yeah, and you'll probably have a better chance of winning the lottery; plus, we'll be explaining why you shot into the hill without knowing what's up there. Fuck it, I think he's gone. Let's get back into the building. We're not safe here," she said as she backed toward the full cover of the building.

# CHAPTER 14

I felt like I had talked to half the VIPD when Lieutenant Dory Hancock finally came up to me. "OK," he said, pulling me aside and away from a uniformed officer who was talking to me and walked me to the dark side of the building away from the crowd of cops and witnesses. "I get it; someone is killing off people connected with this StreGo company." He growled when we were alone. "I also get it that you're working for this StreGo company."

I nodded.

"Look, Mad Dog, most cops would have a beef with you right now, but I got no ego, I got no turf. All I know is this morning, I was working on two murders, and now I think I got murders coming out of the woodwork, and half of them nobody even knew were murders. I know the three of you are way ahead of me in the power curve, so you level with me, and I'll forget all the shit."

"Let us work our case," I said.

Hancock's huge round black face twitched, and, in the darkness, I sensed his massive body tense, "Why?" he asked, his voice firm but confidential.

I looked behind me, sensing I was about to make a deal that no one should hear, and said," Look, I'll level with you, but you're right. You are up to your ass in alligators, and we can work together."

"I won't cover for you if you break the law." He said.

"Agreed, I won't tell you if I break the law."

The big man smiled, "You keep a leash on Jones."

"You know better," I said.

"Will you at least try to keep Ray from doing anything so crazy I end up regretting this?"

"Agreed, I'll try," I said with a smile.

"You keep me in the loop on everything."

"Agreed," I said and put my hand out.

Hancock's massive right hand grabbed mine, and we shook.

"How long will it take before you can leave the scene?" I asked.

"Mr. Cotton, I can leave right now, you see, if there is nobody in a bag," he smiled and pointed at his big square head, "there is no reason for Dory. I just do homicide."

I smiled back.

Dory took his finger away from his head, looked at Cheri, and then back at me, and said, "I bet I can even get the investigating officer to agree to meet with you and Cheri tomorrow. We may have some ballistics or something off the hill. If we do, you will know."

That offer sounded good. I had been standing around for two hours and was ready to gather up Ziggy and Cheri and get as far away from that bush-covered hill and the gas station as possible.

"It's time for me to get Cheri and Ziggy out of here and somewhere safe."

"Done," he said as he walked toward a knot of officers talking to witnesses.

I turned and walked into the gas station. Cheri and Ziggy were inside the gas station's small store. Ziggy was on his fifth beer and beginning to fade.

"We're free to get out of here," I said, waving them toward me. "Let's go."

"We have to be interviewed," Cheri said, registering a slight anger.

"No worries," I said, "My new friend Lieutenant Dory said we can talk to the investigating officer tomorrow."

# CHAPTER 15

Sam True was treading water in his new pool in the elite gated community of Choy. Choy is a group of million-dollar homes facing the Caribbean and is bordered by the Buccaneer resort on one side and Green Key Marina on the other side. Below the pool, the surf washed in and out with the rhythm of the heavy seas banging against the island's north shore.

The water was cool, and the strong sea breeze and warm morning sun felt good on Sam's face. In the morning serenity, a dove's lonesome coo, carried by the breeze, purred across the edges of his consciousness.

Sam opened his eyes and turned toward his house, sitting atop the hill overlooking the sloping lawn and his pool. The house was a monster, with seven bedrooms. Not bad, he thought, for a kid from Kennedy Projects with a 10th-grade education.

With a feeling of contentment, he thought of his delicate wife sleeping quietly in the large four-poster bed, his bed; he smiled to himself; the night before, he had gotten to show off his new bride to his brothers from the gang. He remembered the jealousy and lust in their eyes as they watched her small, tight body serve them beer, and she even teased the bad boys a little. His new wife had been a dancer at the local strip club and knew how to make a man crazy.

The rising sun's warmth reminded him of lying next to his woman. He smiled as he daydreamed of climbing from the pool, toweling off, and going up to enjoy his woman. "Wow," he thought, "who said money can't buy love."

As he turned his face away from the sun's warm rays, he looked at the pool's mirror-like reflection from the large bank of glass that made up the north wall of his home. In the reflection, he noticed the figure standing behind him at the edge of his pool. He was turning in the water to face the figure when he smelled the gas.

# CHAPTER 16

Dory saw Cheri, Ray, and I as we stood outside the new set of crime scene tape. With a wave of Dory's hand, one of the uniforms that was assigned to keep the Looky Lou's off the property escorted the three of us over to where Dory was standing.

"What's up?" Ray asked, offering Dory one of his special homeboy handshakes that white people always fuck up. The two did the slap, flap, jam like they had been practicing for years and offered each other a solemn all business face.

Dory smiled and offered his hand to Cheri, and she smiled back in a "this is a murder scene" kind of serious way. He then offered me his hand and I shook it. "What, no bro flip, slap, tap for the white guy?" I thought.

Dory released my hand and pulled a white sheet of paper from his suit pocket. I recognized it as a list of all the StreGo owners from tiers one through three. He made a show of putting on the glasses he had taken from his coat pocket and ran his sausage-sized index finger down the page. "Sam True," he said, looking up at me, the noon sun reflecting off the glasses.

"Tier two," I said.

"Yep," Ray said.

"Tier two," Dory confirmed, folding the paper, and putting it back in his pocket. He then slowly, deliberately took off the reading glasses, studied them for a second, and slid them back into the suit pocket with the list.

"Sam True," Cheri said, making a slight point with her head toward the huge pink house.

"How," I asked.

"Come see," Dory said and turned and began to walk toward the mansion. Like three little ducks in a line, we followed.

Dory took us through the six-car garage, which was empty except for a new red Jeep Grand Cherokee, and back into the rear of the house. Most of the VIPD brass stood in a huddle about forty feet from a large reflection pool.

At the pool, Sergeant Al Lester stood at the edge of the water, taking a sample. His boss, the head forensic investigator Morty Felix, was taking photos of a body floating face down in the pool.

Dory caught Morty's eye and waved him over. "Hi guys," Morty said as he walked over and raised his gloved hands showing he couldn't shake.

"Hi Morty," Cheri said, "I thought you were retired."

"Kids in school," he said.

"Should have thought of that before you had so many," Ray said, giving Morty a nudge.

Morty gave Ray an old friend smile and said, "I'm just glad none of them are yours."

"Ray returned the smile," and gave Morty what was probably a wink from behind his Ray Bans.

"Tell these guys what you told me," Dory said, getting down to business.

"Well," Morty said, "We won't know until the doctor does the autopsy for sure, but I'm pretty sure Mr. True was enjoying a morning swim when some less-than-friendly soul poured gas in his lovely pool and set it on fire." He motioned toward a red, plastic five-gallon can that was tipped on its side on the far side of the pool.

I looked over at the pool and looked more closely at the body in the pool.

"I figure the perp poured the gas in the pool and lit it off," Morty said with an upward wave of his hands.

"Is he burnt?" I asked.

"Nope, the water protected most of his body, but every hair on his head is singed off."

"Probably affixation," Dory said, "You know, big breath of super-hot air," he added.

"Minor burns, I think, on the back of the neck, the head, and back, but our victim is a black man, so it's harder to tell without a closer examination, and I don't want to screw with the body till Doc Matrix gets here."

"How would the perp sneak up on the guy and pour gas in the pool without him knowing?" I asked.

"Held him at gunpoint, maybe," Ray said.

"I'd still be scrambling out," Dory said, "better shot than burnt."

"Me too," I agreed, thinking of that moment you saw the gas going into the pool and the raw terror that it would cause.

"The perp might not have even let Mr. True know he was there," Cheri motioned east. With the wind, if he was sitting in his pool watching the sun come up, he might not have known anyone was there until he smelled the gas."

Morty looked at the pool for a long time and then said in a quiet voice, "The poor guy wouldn't have known there was anything wrong until the gas was around him."

"Cold," Ray said, looking at the pool.

"Cold either way, "Cheri agreed, "It takes a lot of hate to burn a man to death."

"No," Dory said, "The other sin, greed killed this man."

"I wonder where my coroner is," Dory said, looking at his watch.

Like entering on cue, Doctor Sally Matrix walked through the garage door and down the lawn toward our little group. Doctor Matrix was dressed in blue coveralls with a small patch that announced the Virgin Islands Coroner's office. In her right hand, she carried a large tan and white fishing tackle box. In her left hand, she carried a brown leather satchel. Behind her trailed two large men, also in blue coveralls.

The straight starched lines of the coveralls could not hide Dr. Matrix's long, athletic figure. Although we had been friends for years, she was all business as she ignored Ray, Cheri, and me. She headed straight for Dory and extended her hand. "Good morning," she said.

Dory looked at his watch and said, "Good afternoon, Doc."

"Sorry, I'm a little late. I was in autopsies when you called."

St. Croix shares a forensic examiner with St. Thomas and St. John. Doctor Sally Matrix is the forensic examiner for the whole Territory of the United States Virgin Islands and usually comes to St. Croix once a week if an autopsy has to be performed or she has to testify in a case.

"I'm just glad you were on the island, "Felix said, pointing at the body in the pool, "This is one where you will probably want to see the scene."

Sally looked over at the pool, turned away from us, and started to walk toward it. Her two helpers and Felix scurried after her, carrying an array of cameras, lights, and large tackle boxes.

"I gotta go," Dory said as he turned and followed.

As Dory walked away, Ray turned his back to me and began talking to Cheri.

Suddenly, I felt alone. I turned toward the east and looked out over the view of Buck Island. In the distance to the north, I could see the clear outlines of St. Thomas, St. John, and the British Virgin Islands on the horizon. The strong wind was beginning to slow, but the breeze still made the large multi-color Bougainvillea bushes sway. As I watched the patterns of orange and red Bougainvillea flowers dance in front of the perfect tones of the blue and green white-capped sea, I wondered how something as vile as burning a man to death could exist in the same place that such beauty existed.

On the patio above the pool, I saw two female officers sitting quietly with a small black woman in a large white terry cloth robe. I looked at Dory, and he said with a sad shake of his head, "This guy got married just last week. That's his new bride."

He looked at the pool and continued, "The gardener found the body and called the police. I had to wake her and tell her that her new husband was dead; some days, I hate this job." Dory said with a shake of his head

I looked back across the perfectly manicured lawn and up the hill at the patio and felt a sadness for the small, almost child-like woman. It was the wrong time to interview the victim's wife, but I felt a need to, at the very least, give her my condolences.

I told Ray and Cheri I was going up for water and would bring one down to them. They nodded and continued viewing the scene deep in their own discussion.

As I walked up the hill, I knew that even the slight intrusion of offering my condolences to the new bride was wrong and selfish. As I reached the patio, I had a choice: I could veer toward the open back door of the house or turn toward the three women sitting at the patio table.

I heard a large policewoman who had her hand on Tam True's hand patting it, "Just relax Tam, it'll pass."

"I feel sick, sick inside like my insides are black like they're dying," the widow said, laying her head on the big woman's shoulder.

"Just relax, Tam," the other officer said, lightly stroking her back.

"Oh god, "the small woman wailed, "I feel like the smell is inside me. I can't get the smell of burning hair out of my mind. Oh god, that smell, it's like it's in me." As she broke into a low moan, the two officers pulled her into a protective hug.

Talking to the widow at that moment was wrong. I veered toward the open door and emotional safety of the kitchen to get the waters.

## CHAPTER 17

We left the crime scene around noon, and the three of us met at Maria's Cantina for lunch and to regroup. Ray got to the restaurant first and got us a table outside. When Cheri and I found him, he was feeding the chickens tortilla chips and had already gathered two hens, about five chicks, and one very henpecked rooster.

"Jesus, Ray," Cheri said, taking a slow kick at a rooster that charged under her feet for one of the chips.

"Always starting shit," I said, eyeing three brightly dressed senior citizens that were glaring at our table like we were lepers escaping from our assigned colony. I eyed the three cute little cue tips and gave a slight wave, and they quickly turned their attention back to their afternoon margaritas.

Ray raised the Coors light he was drinking and took a long drink, ignoring everyone and watching the chickens. "You know," he said, "between new murders and people with iron-clad alibis, we're running through our list of good suspects pretty fast."

"I think we need to make a matrix of the first three tiers of StreGo owners and start making our way down the list," Cheri said, pulling a typewritten list of the owners out of her black Mickey Mouse carry bag.

"Seems like a good start," I said, looking over at Ray.

"What if there is more than one person doing the murders, or they have a hired killer," Ray asked.

"Then we will get tripped up a little, but we just need to keep that little possibility in mind," I said as the waitress approached our table.

"Ray," the waitress said with a fake scowl, "you know better than feeding the chickens."

Ray looked at the three ladies, who were now ignoring us, and said, "They squeal on me?"

"Nope," she said with a winning smile, "but you just confessed."

"Whoops," he said, raising both hands.

"Can you two keep him under control?" She asked Cheri and I.

"You're the second person to ask us that today," Cheri said.

"Big surprise," the waitress said, slapping Ray on the shoulder and then asking what we wanted.

We ordered, and as the waitress walked away, I asked, "One of your many fans?"

"Nope, my cousin on my mom's side."

Cheri pulled out the list of owners for StreGo and laid it on the table. "How should we do this?" she said, looking down at the page.

Ray looked at the list and shook his head, "We're talking a lot of money, but I can't believe someone would kill this many people just for money."

Cheri started putting an "x" next to all the people we had talked to who had iron-clad alibis for one or more of the murders and the shooting at Ziggy's. We were able to eliminate about half of the people on the first and second group of owners, but we still had a lot of interviews.

"We need to think about what else we know about the killer or killers," I said.

"Well, I'll tell ya one thing," Ray said, "Whoever did the shooting at Martin's office was seriously good. Two shots to the head and caught both sitting in their chairs, that's not easy."

"I agree," I said, and I'll bet you a hundred dollars that the shot from the hill was designed to break that bottle and rattle us, not kill anyone."

Ray nodded, and Cheri said, "Why do you think that?"

"Just a gut feeling," I said, sitting back and wondering why Ray's cousin hadn't brought out our waters and fresh tortilla chips; my stomach gave an angry roll and grumbled.

"I can't put my finger on it, but I feel the same way," Ray said, taking a final sip of his beer. "Something tells me this guy is good at what he's doing, really good."

"Enough money in this to hire a professional," Cheri said.

I raised my hand and held up one finger. "Cop," I raised a second finger. " Soldier," I continued, "ex-cop, ex-soldier, nobody else gets that kind of training."

"Thug," Ray said, raising one finger.

"Thug," I agreed.

"Whoever it is, they have killed by a car, burning, gunshot, both pistol and high powered rifle and if our killer also got Terry Jeffery, maybe another method," Cheri said.

"And if Jeffery is a victim why hide him and none of the rest?" I asked.

"The hit and run is a high-risk way to kill someone, as is walking into a law office, but the shot at Ziggy's is sneaky. These murders are all over the board," Ray said, "no pattern."

"The only real pattern is the victims," I said.

As Ray's cousin approached with the food, we stopped talking, and Cheri folded the sheet of paper and dropped it into her purse.

# CHAPTER 18

If you think there is any glamour in being an investigator, you're wrong. It's usually just lots of leg work, and this case was becoming pure leg work. Ray had returned to his "protection" of Cindy Childers but promised to start putting in time as soon as he could get Cindy in a completely safe environment. Considering the motive to kill her and the history of the murders, I figured that the only safe place must be the moon.

After some debate and considering the incident at Ziggy's, Cheri and I decided that working together, although it would be slower, would be safer, and having two people observe the people we interviewed would be helpful.

After some phone calls, we set up meetings with four of the StreGo second-tier owners. The first one we were set to visit was Collin Roberts. According to the sheet Martin had given us, Collin owned 4% of the second tier. The 4% interest showed he had not purchased any additional ownership or brought other investors into the company.

Collin was a postman and agreed to take a break and meet us at the Gallows Bay coffee shop. The coffee shop is in the same small strip mall as Maria's Cantina, so after lunch, Cheri and I just walked to the end of the mall and took seats outside the coffee shop.

We only had to wait about 5 minutes, and a small postal van pulled into the parking lot and parked. Collin Roberts stepped out of the van, and Cheri waved to get his attention. With a small wave, he started toward our table.

Mr. Roberts was a tall, slender man. I guessed he was easily six foot six but probably weighed less than a hundred and eighty pounds. He wore the standard postman-issue uniform, which was starched, and all the creases were sharp and exact. His dark hair was cut short, and a faint hint of gray was beginning to appear at the tip of his short sideburns.

When he reached our table he extended his hand with a smile to Cheri and said, "Good afternoon, I'm Collin." His speech carried the hint of British formality that is common among the people who are originally from the British Islands of the Caribbean.

After shaking Cheri's hand, he turned to me and shook my hand. His handshake and smile were genuine; he was one of those people who immediately made you feel comfortable and relaxed. "And you're the Mad Dog Cotton that I have heard so much of," he said as he folded into the chair across from us.

"All good stuff, I hope," I said.

He gave me an easy smile, waved his hand, and said, "Oh yes, Tony and Madge Taylor are good friends. They told me how you and Cheri helped Ray Jones get their daughter back after she was kidnapped. I would say, at least in the eyes of that family, you are somewhat of a hero."

I was somewhat at a loss for words and said, "The Taylors are good people. How are they doing?"

"Great, as a matter of fact. Susan has just been accepted into the National Honor Society and is going to

Washington D.C. for some kind of national award ceremony."

I remembered the tough and smart girl we had helped the year before and had to smile.

"She's a great kid," Cheri said, "how do you know the Taylor's."

"Tony and I are like brothers. Our fathers came to St. Croix back in the seventies from Dominica to work out at the refinery out at Hovensa."

"Dominica," I said, "I thought I heard a little of that British accent."

"Ah yes, we are a little more formal than our Cruzan friends," he said before he asked, "So, how can I help you two?"

"Well, actually, Mr. Taylor," Cheri started,

"Collin, please," he interrupted with another full-toothed smile.

"Well, Collin, we actually want to talk to you about StreGo."

Collin Roberts's mood seemed to darken, and he sat back slightly in his chair and laced his hands in front of him. "StreGo?" he asked.

"Yes," Cheri went on, "Ray Jones, Mad Dog, and I have been hired to look into the deaths of some of StreGo's owners."

"I see," he said; his demeanor had gone from friendly to guarded as he leaned further back and folded his long, slender arms.

"We understand that you are one of the owners on the second level of StreGo." Cheri continued.

"I am."

"I know this is uncomfortable, but we are trying to learn as much about the company as possible," Cheri said. I could tell she was trying to understand and adjust to Collin's change in attitude.

"It's not uncomfortable, Mrs. Cotton," he said, formalizing each word. It is quite simply a very, very difficult subject for me."

"Can you explain?" Cheri asked.

"Explain," he said, his voice turning thoughtful. After a long pause, he said, "Madge Thomas, like Tony, is from Dominica."

"I didn't know that," Cheri said.

"Madge and I have been close friends for the last 40 years. Mike, Charlie's dad, was the best man at my wedding. After Mike died and left Madge and Charlie alone, I took little Charlie under my wing."

"Since Mike's death, I have felt a," he paused as if considering his words, "responsibility for Madge and Charlie. You see, Mike and I had a fishing boat together. We would go fishing on weekends to make a little extra cash. I couldn't go one weekend, so Mike went out alone. No one knows what happened, but a dive boat found our fishing boat floating off Buck Island, and Mike has not been seen since. I have always felt it was my fault and that Mike would still be with us if I had been there."

"How long ago did Mike die?" I asked.

The postman's eyes fluttered from side to side for a moment, and he seemed lost in thought. Then, in a soft voice, he said, "1993, November 17, 1993, Charlie was still in grade school, and Madge," he paused, and his eyes began to water. Madge was an at-home mom. Mike was a supervisor at Hovensa by then and making good money. Our lives seemed so perfect, so promising."

Collin Roberts pulled the thin fingers of his long hand across his eyes, wiping the moister away. "Life and happiness are a fragile thing," he said, his voice still soft, his eyes still distant, "In Dominica, life had been hard, and our lives in St. Croix were like a fairy tale. We were family; we did everything together; we worked, played, and dreamed together. Mike and I dreamed of fishing for a living, buying a charter boat, and fishing for marlin and sailfish. It was a good dream, a good life."

"Is that why you invested in StreGo?" Cheri asked.

"Yes," he said as his posture seemed to relax again. Madge came to me a couple of years ago and told me about the company that Charlie was trying to put together and asked if I would invest in it. It was a lot of money, and I'm not the investment type, but I could never say no to Madge. So, I invested ten thousand dollars in Charlie's company."

"Pretty good investment," I said.

Again, Collin seemed to tense. "Financially, yes,"

"You're aware that some of the owners of StreGo have died recently," Cheri asked.

"I'm sorry," he said. "I don't know who any of the investors are other than Charlie and Madge. I know Charlie is dead, of course. Also, I knew that the lawyer, Mr. Shields, was an owner; Madge told me he was working for a share of the company when I went in to sign my agreement.

"In the last two months, five of the initial investors in StreGo have died suspiciously, "I said, "including Martin Shields."

Collin Roberts sat still, looking more through me than at me.

"StreGo has six primary investors," Cheri said. "Four of them have been killed."

"Killed?" Collin said, his dark coffee-colored skin seeming to blanch.

"We believe murdered," I said.

He looked at me, his face without expression, and said, "Why."

"Mr. Roberts," Cheri said softly, "We believe that someone is killing owners of StreGo to gain control of the company."

He turned his gaze toward Cheri and, for a very long moment, seemed to be digesting what she was saying. He then seemed to focus and said, "Is Madge in any danger?"

"There is no way to be sure, Mr. Roberts, but we believe that the motive is to take control of the company, and Madge has no interest in the company. She sold it all some time back."

"Yes, "he said, now fully focused on Cheri, "Madge told me she had sold her interest in the company; I think when Charlie died, it ripped her heart out. She gave the money she got for her interest in the company to the church. She told me about the drugs in the formula and told me I should sell my shares, but frankly, when those big checks started coming in, I just couldn't justify selling, even though Madge told me I should. My wife and I have worked our whole lives, and now the money from the company is like a godsend."

He paused to get his thoughts together and then continued, "Am I in danger? Is my wife?"

Cheri and I looked at each other, and she said, "Possibly."

Collin took a deep breath and let it out slowly, "She," he paused, "My wife is my life. Should we leave? Should we leave the island?"

I thought about the question—the nightmare of being forced to leave your home because of a psychopath's actions. In my gut, I knew that if I were Collin Roberts, I would take Cheri and run, but who was I to tell this man to run from his life, friends, and job?

"Leave," he said softly like he was exploring the word.

I was beginning to nod my head when Cheri said in a low but solid voice, "Collin if I were you, I would drive home, pack a bag, and fly out of St. Croix on the next flight."

"Leave," he repeated in a dead voice as the emotion in his long, wrinkled face went flat.

Cheri reached across the table and held Collin's hand. "Mr. Roberts, there has been a string of deaths we believe were murders of StreGo owners. I know this is hard, but I can tell you that if I were a StreGo owner, I would already be on a plane."

"I have to go," he said in a dazed voice.

Cheri nodded and said, "Mr. Roberts, before you go, can I ask you a few more questions?"

Collin Robert's gaze was far away. Then he made a small headshake, and his attention centered back on Cheri. "If I can help you in any way, any way at all, I will, but please, I have to go right now. My wife is home and alone."

"Two questions,"

He nodded and sat back in the chair his large body shrinking into the chair.

"When did Madge tell you about the drugs in the protein's formula?"

"Madge loved Charlie, but the use of steroids in his protein powder, she couldn't tolerate that, not after all her years on the force."

I looked at Cheri, and she gave me a quick glance.

"Years on the force?" I asked.

"Yeah, Madge was an officer at VIPD for 16 years. After Mike died, I helped her get a job as a clerk at VIPD, and the next year, she applied for the academy. She breezed through the academy, graduated, and became a uniformed officer. She surprised us all. She went from a quiet, shy woman to a" he stopped and smiled "to a super cop. She worked the street for two years and then went into vice. She was in vice for most of that time before the Chief moved her to Robbery Homicide just before Charlie died."

"Madge Thomas was a cop?" I asked.

"Yeah," Collin said, his voice regaining some of its strength, "and a damn good one."

"She's Sergeant Thomas?" Cheri asked.

"Yeah." He said.

"The Sergeant Thomas?" Cheri said.

"Yep," Collin said, a touch of pride in his voice. "M. L. Thomas."

A few years earlier, I remembered the name from the papers: "I always thought that Sergeant Thomas was a guy." I said.

"Yeah, a lot of people thought so because she could kick some serious ass."

I remembered reading multiple articles about the exploits of Sergeant M.L. Thomas, "She single-handedly shot and arrested the three guys who were robbing the First Bank." I said, my mind racing.

"Yep," Collin said with his first smile since our conversation had gone so serious, "also drove her car into that corrupt Judge Jamison's airplane when he tried to fly off the island."

"That was her?" I said, thinking of the stern schoolteacher type of personality I had assigned to her when we met.

"Yep," Collin said, "and she had a lot more crazy stunts she pulled over the years."

"I never put it together," Cheri said, looking stunned, "When I was a Marshal, I heard her name a hundred times, but I never realized that Sergeant Thomas was a woman."

Collin gave Cheri a huge smile and shook his head, "Mike was six foot six and spent eight years in the National Guard, and I saw her whip his ass twice." He gave a small laugh and shook his head, "God help your little murderer if he decides to mess with that girl."

I smiled at the pure pride in Collin's voice. "If you're leaving, sir," I said, "can we get your phone number when we have other questions?"

"Yeah," he said as he reached into his pocket and handed me a card. "My wife printed these out for me. You're the first person I have ever given one of these to."

"Thanks," Cheri said, taking the card. Collin stretched his long frame out of the chair and stepped back.

"Thanks for the warning," he said. I mean, if I hadn't talked to you guys, my wife and I could have…" He stopped and got quiet for a long time, then looked back up at us and just said, "Thanks." Then he turned and walked in long, fast strides toward the little postal van.

As he drove away, Cheri said, "he's gonna be OK."

"I hope so, "I said, "he seems like a hell of a nice guy."

"We need to look at Madge Thomas, Cheri," I said.

"No shit, she has all the skill sets. She may blame the victims for her son's death or something." She said, her voice far away.

# CHAPTER 19

When we pulled up to Madge's house, she was again in her garden. We parked, and I looked out across the garden at our suspect. She had on a bright flowered T-shirt and faded Levis. On her head, she wore a bright pink sombrero-type hat. When she saw us, she stood and started toward us.

"Be careful," Cheri said as she climbed out," this bitch can be a lot more dangerous than she looks."

I touched the weight of my Glock on my hip and smiled, "Don't worry, baby, I don't mind shooting old ladies who are serial killers."

She smiled and hopped out of the truck greeting Madge with a smile and, "Mrs. Thomas, where were you yesterday morning."

Stopping in mid-stride, Madge smiled at Cheri and pulled off her gloves. After tucking her gloves in her hip pocket, she said, "Good morning, now, Mrs. Cotton. You know that is the proper greeting. Why so rude?"

"Answer the question," Cheri said in a tone that was all business.

"Yesterday," she replied calmly, touching her right hand to her chin as if thinking, "I was at the Baptist Church from 5:00 a.m. until 3:00 p.m. working on the bake sale, and you, my dear, where were you?"

"Do you remember Sam True?" Cheri shot back.

The woman absently scratched and pulled a piece of dead skin from her neck. She examined the particle in her fingers and flicked it away. She was silent for a second, and then her right hand rose and rested on her chin, and in a thoughtful voice, she said, "Sam True, yes, I do remember that little maggot."

"You didn't like him?" Cheri said again all business.

"Oh goodness no, Sam True was a low-life piece of shit, "she said with a smile. "I have to confess I was elated to hear from Detective Morris that someone tried to boil him in his nice new swimming pool."

"Morris called you?" I asked.

"Of course, dear, Mike was my partner at VIPD. He always calls me when one of the real scum gets checked off. He knows it makes my day."

Madge Thomas's words were completely inconsistent with her grandmother's look and friendly tone. I had to take a second to process what she had just said.

"You were at church yesterday morning?" I said.

"Yes, dear, call my pastor. I got there early to set up for the bake sale. We use the large oven at the church to cook, and the crowd loves my cinnamon rolls, so I bake a couple hundred." She smiled a big granny smile that showed a full set of white teeth. "They do like my rolls," she finished.

"Sorry I was so rude," Cheri said.

"I understand, honey." Madge said, looking Cheri in the eye sternly, "You thought I might have killed Mr. True and maybe even all those other owners of Charlie's company. I was a detective for twelve years, and I know what it's like to have a suspect in a homicide. Actually, I was expecting you to ask me about the killings the other day."

"We hadn't put two and two together the other day," I said.

She smiled, "You mean cop and mother of the company's founder?"

"Yeah," Cheri said.

"Well, you two seem very good at what you're doing. I'm glad I was at church yesterday, so you didn't feel obligated to make some kind of a citizen's arrest." She said as she absently rubbed the rash on her neck and flicked another fleck of skin away.

"I've got some great cream for that," Cheri said, gesturing at the rash that spread around Madge's neck.

"No worry, child," she said. "Too much time in the sun, but thanks."

I had to smile at her, "Word is you were hell on wheels," I said.

"Still am, honey," she said, patting what I realized was a small gun in the front pocket of her jeans, "you two need a little backup; give me a call. I miss getting to kick the shit out of the maggots that are fucking with my island."

# CHAPTER 20

"Jesus Christ," I said, climbing back into the truck.

"Kicking the shit of the maggots, I can't believe she said that," Cheri said, "That was like going into a scene of the God Mother."

"What a great suspect," I said.

"Yeah," Cheri agreed, "but if her alibi sticks, she's just one more to cross off the list."

I called Ray, put my phone on speaker, and told him about our meeting with Madge Thomas. He began to laugh. "I'd have paid money to be there, Sergeant Thomas and you two. I've known Madge since she started on the force and busted me for disturbing the peace. I love that old lady."

"Why didn't you say something?" I asked.

"I didn't realize what you two were up to," he laughed again. Man, oh man, what a sight—a gunfight in the old lady's garden. I will have to keep closer tabs on you two, or you'll be trying to put the cuffs on the mayor next."

"Well, maybe when you quit playing house, you'll have time to keep us out of trouble," Cheri said.

"Strange you should mention that," Ray said. I'm putting Cindy on a plane today for Atlanta, and then you and I can start figuring this out. If you want to have a little fun later today, I thought we could go have a heart-to-heart with my old friend Antonio Mendoza. I consider him my number one suspect in this little case."

Antonio Mendoza owned over one-third of the tier three profits, plus he would be one of the owners of profits from the production plant in Puerto Rico and stood to control foreign franchise rights of the StreGo product if the last two original owners were killed. In short, with Sonny and Ziggy out of the way, his financial gain would be huge. When I added the fact that Antonio Mendoza controlled a criminal organization that was more than capable of committing all the murders we were investigating, he had to be our key suspect.

"Let's face it," Cheri said, "Mendoza is our number one suspect, but damn tough to prove because he can order all these killings and keep his hands clean."

"Yep," said Ray, "also, if he has his boys doing the deeds, that explains the different styles of killing."

"How do we talk to him?" I asked, ready to get after my second perfect suspect of the day.

"Simple," Ray said, "I make a phone call, and the three of us drive up to his little mansion on the hill and share some quality time."

"I'll call John, "Cheri said.

"Good plan," I said. John Canfield was Cheri's partner when she was a Federal Marshal. In the past, when we needed backup, we could always rely on John.

# CHAPTER 21

Ray dropped Cindy off for her six o'clock flight and met us at the boat at five-thirty. When he finally climbed on the boat, Cheri, John, and I were on the flybridge drinking coffee and discussing the safest way to meet Antonio Mendoza.

After a few minutes of small talk, we settled down to business.

Ray unrolled a three-month-old Google Earth aerial photo of a group of houses. "Mendoza has purchased an old plantation compound just west of Mutual Homes by the Botanical Gardens. He has turned it into kind of a clubhouse for a lot of the Mutual Homes guys, so we can expect a lot of hostile souls in and around the compound if our little talk goes bad."

"How many guys?" John asked.

"Hard to tell, but the guy I talked with seemed to think no less than seven, depending on who's in and out of jail."

"Armed?" I asked.

"Most likely," Ray said, "The boys from Mutual Homes drove out to Lorain Village last week and did a drive-by. I'm pretty sure the guys at Lorain will retaliate. The question is when an attack on Antonio's little compound would be expected, so the short answer to your question is, yeah, the boys around Antonio's compound will be armed to the teeth."

"You really think that meeting with Mendoza will help in any way?" John asked.

Ray smiled and shrugged, "Can't hurt."

"They shoot you, or whoever goes with you, I can guarantee it will hurt," John said, giving Ray a big smile.

"For all gain, you must risk pain," Ray said, returning John's smile.

"For all gain, you must risk pain," I interrupted. " You find that in a fortune cookie?"

"Bathroom wall more likely," Cheri said, giving Ray a playful punch.

"Seriously, guys, this is a dangerous deal; Antonio Mendoza has killed or ordered the killing of dozens of people on this island. I don't trust him, and unless we got one hell of a lot to gain, I think going into that compound is crazy," John said

"I tend to agree," said Cheri.

"OK," I said, "show them, Ray."

Ray ducked his head, kicked his foot to the side like a scolded school kid, and said, "Aw come on, Mad Dog, it'll wreck the surprise."

"Show them," I said.

Ray lit up like a schoolchild and pulled a small wooden box from his jeans pocket. The box looked like teak and was the size of a ring box.

"You're gonna propose?" Cheri asked, looking at the box.

"Yep," Ray said, "Propose we bug Antonio's office with this." He opened the box, exposing a pea-sized silver oval.

"Bug," John said.

"Thousand dollars' worth of bug," Ray said, passing the bug around. On closer observation, the bug looked like a silver stickpin.

"In his clubhouse," I said, "Ray talked to one of the guys who used to be in Antonio's Posse. He likes to hold court in his clubhouse and issue orders in front of his boys. If he orders another killing of a StreGo owner, Ray and I believe he will do it from that main room in the clubhouse."

"What an arrogant ass hole," Cheri said with a shake of her head.

"Yeah," Ray agreed, "arrogant as hell, but we will let that arrogance pay us dividends. This little bug is completely amazing. It will pick up everything that happens in that room, and all we need is to get his plan and catch him red-handed, either doing the deed or paying to have it done."

I picked up the stick pin and examined it. On the device, there was a half-inch-long pin with a barb-like texture. "You just push it into a couch and start listening."

Ray nodded and said, "I think planting this bug makes our trip to Mendoza worth the risk."

Cheri looked at Ray for a long while and then at John, "It's worth the risk," she said.

"Only Ray and I are going in. You two need to cover our backs." I said.

Cheri looked at me for a long moment, her lips pursed as if she wanted to say something. Then, she slowly let the air out of her lungs. "Just in and out." She said.

"If Antonio has an audience of his boys, he may get loud or obnoxious, but I really doubt he'll get violent. He's too savvy to do something that dumb." I said.

"So, we're on protection detail again," John said, giving Cheri a pat on the back.

"Yep," She said, "Ray, will you help John and I do a recon on this property so we have it down."

"Yep," Ray said, "How about we do a recon tonight and tomorrow, Mad Dog and I will make our visit."

# CHAPTER 22

Antonio Mendoza's newly purchased property consisted of a large pink colonial-era home and a dozen outbuildings. From the cover of the bush across from the closest outbuilding, a roofless stone structure, I could hear the party in the main house.

The area was a chaotic shamble. The stone building that blocked my view of the main house and the driveway that was the only entrance into the property was covered with the remains of what looked like a hundred years of litter. Corners or squares of tin that were probably the remains of roofs ripped free by a forgotten hurricane were mixed with the remains of thousands of cans, bottles, and loose papers. On the side of the ruined building, someone had stacked an old mattress that, after years in the elements, was a dark, soiled brown.

The ground between the small stone building and our hiding place was brown, hard-packed soil with a layer of cans and bottles that made moving further into the compound without making a sound impossible.

"Jesus," Ray said, moving beside me, "I smell something dead."

I took a tentative sniff, and the faint but undeniable scent of death seeped into my senses. "This place is a war zone," I whispered as I tried to figure out how to get to the small stone house without being heard to get a good look at the rest of the compound.

"You try to crawl, and the broken glass is gonna shred your hands, and the trash is gonna let them know you're coming from a mile away," Ray said.

It had taken the four of us nearly an hour to move through a quarter mile of bush that surrounded the compound, and now that we were at the edge of the compound, our efforts seemed to be in vain. To our right was a deep ravine covered with old trash ranging from an old truck frame to huge piles of common garbage thrown for years into the ravine. Thirty yards to our left was a natural wall of thorn bush that seemed to run back into the bush for hundreds of yards.

"There's a trail that runs from the Marley Project to the house that the home boys use, but if we use it, the chances of running into some gun-toting trigger happy sixteen-year-old are pretty good," Ray said.

"Sorry to say it, but I'm short on ideas, "I said, "I want to see the area so we at least have a plan tomorrow when we drive in here, but this bush is so thick there's no way we can have John and Cheri cover us once we get into the compound."

From behind us in the dark shadows of the bush, John cloaked in a full suit of dark camouflage, whispered," I have an idea."

Ray and I turned and moved back from the edge of the clearing to where Cheri and John were waiting.

"What you got, Big Guy," I said when I was close enough to see John's heavy outline.

"I think it will be easier to show you than tell you," he said, "so follow me."

We followed John back into the tangle of thick bush we had just emerged from until we came to a small clearing. The clearing surrounded a huge tree, and John pointed at it.

"Damn nice breadfruit tree," Cheri said, looking up into the thick branches of the huge tree.

"I think we can climb it." John said, "Get up high enough to get a good look at the compound."

"It may be high enough to give us a view," Cheri said.

"And if I can get up there, I'll be able to give you guys good cover if your little visit turns to shit."

"I don't climb," Ray said, his voice flat.

I looked at the huge, ancient tree and said, "Once you get to the limbs, I could see you climbing in the branches, but the trunk has to be thirty feet up before you get to the branches."

"Not easy," John said.

"I don't climb," Ray repeated.

"Ladder," Cheri said more to herself.

"Rope," I said, wondering if I could throw a coil of rope over the lowest limb.

Cheri approached the tree and began to examine the trunk, "Look," she said.

The three of us gathered around us and examined the trunk.

"I'll be damned," I said, looking at huge nails that had been driven into the trunk of the tree.

"These were driven into the side of the tree to allow people to climb the tree and get to the breadfruit,"

I grabbed one of the huge rust-coated nails and pulled on it. It was solid. "They seem to be solid," I said.

"I bet someone used to consider this their private breadfruit stash," Cheri said.

Ray stepped up and examined the nails that stuck out from the giant tree about five inches." I bet these were pounded into this tree a hundred years ago; I bet no one has even been to the base of this tree in years; it's so deep in the bush that it's been completely forgotten.

I looked up into the blackness of the limbs that towered above me, and in the shadows, I could see dozens of the basketball-sized orbs I knew were ripe breadfruit ready for harvest. "If someone knew about this tree, all those breadfruit would be picked," I said, pointing at the round shadows.

"Let's see if we can climb it," John said.

"I don't climb," Ray said for the third time.

I looked at Ray and said, "Scared."

In the deep darkness of the bush, only Ray's eyes could be seen, but those two orbs spoke volumes, and the menace that bore out of his eyes said, "Don't push it."

"Let's give it a try," I said but John was already hoisting his huge bulk up on the first rung of the tree's ancient nail ladder.

We watched him climb until the black-green camouflage of his clothing disappeared into the darkness above us. "This is cool as shit," a voice came from above.

"Shush," Cheri said.

"Sorry," came a whisper from above.

I started up the tree next. The climb was much easier than it had looked. The large nails made for easy climbing and they were cemented into the side of the tree. As I reached the first huge branch of the tree and hooked my body over the limb's girth, I saw the full moon clearly through the tree's foliage.

"Cool as shit," John said from the branch above me.

I looked up, and John sat like a school kid, his back against the tree trunk, staring at the moon.

"Yep," I said.

A second later, Cheri appeared next to me. Her eyes were twinkling with joy. "This is amazing. I'm going up," she said as she moved past me and up the stairs of branches that formed a near walkway up the massive canopy.

I joined her on a thigh-thick branch about sixty feet above the ground. After I settled in, she took my hand and gave me a light kiss. "I feel like a kid." She said.

I wrapped my arms around her and sat looking out over the island. You could see the lights of the Queen Mary Highway to the south and the upper floors of the Marley housing project to the east. A faint hint of a reggae tune flavored the air, and the sweet smell of the ocean breeze filled my lungs. I squeezed Cheri and savored the magic of the moment.

Cheri pointed down at Mendoza's compound. "Not a bad view," she said.

Not two hundred yards in front of us spread Antonio Mendoza's compound. Through the main house window, I saw five men playing cards.

John said above us, "I can cover you guys from here like the hand of god."

"No shit, "I said, considering the hell a sniper could play on the open compound.

From below, Ray said in a loud whisper, "Let's go."

# CHAPTER 23

Antonio Mendoza had agreed to meet with Ray and I at his compound at two in the afternoon. The only stipulation the gang leader had insisted on was no weapons. He said he would be glad to talk to us about StreGo and would supply the beer.

Ray's big truck rolled slowly over the rut-filled road into the compound. Twice he had to come to a complete stop and back up to negotiate the road. "If they ever want to arrest Mendoza, they better bring a half-track," Ray said just as we cleared the trees and pulled into the large cleared area in front of the main house.

In the light of day, the scarred pink stone walls of the house looked shabby and moldy. I realized that the large window through which we had seen the men playing cards had no glass, and the wood molding around it was rotted and partially gone. The front door was composed of heavy mahogany, but years of neglect left it scarred and pitted.

As we pulled up, Antonio Mendoza walked casually out of the front door. He was a short, thin man. He wore dark jeans and a dirty, torn Bob Marley tee shirt. His hair had an almost reddish tint in the strong mid-day sun. It was made up of well-maintained dreadlocks that must have taken hours to braid. His hair hung in a clump as wide as his head. The long dreads were tied together by a long leather strap and the rope of hair swung from side to side as he walked casually toward us.

The most arresting feature of the man was his eyes. Antonio Mendoza's eyes were pale blue and stood out like beacons in contrast to his smooth brown skin. Like pale lasers, his eyes locked on mine and seemed to be searching my soul for a brief second. His gaze was intense, as if, for that brief second, understanding me was the most important thing in the world. As quickly as his laser-like inspection had locked on to me, it left me and turned to Ray.

"Good afternoon, Mr. Jones," he said in a slight Spanish accent.

He offered his hand in a polite and respectful way with a very slight bow. Ray stopped and leaned slightly forward to take the man's hand.

"Good afternoon, Mr. Mendoza," Ray said with a slight smile. Even though Ray's dark wraparound glasses covered his eyes, Mendoza gave Ray the same piercing scrutiny he had given me.

"Mr. Cotton," he said, turning his pale blue eyes back to me and offering me his hand, "welcome."

His handshake was firm but not aggressive, and his smile seemed genuine. "This man is not what I expected," I thought as I turned my eyes to Ray. He gave me an emotionless look that would have made any poker player proud.

"I believe you want to talk about my business interest in StreGo," he said as he released my hand and gestured toward a picnic table on the South side of the open driveway in front of the main house.

"Come, let's sit," he said, gesturing to the bench seats, "I believe that if we sit here in the open, your friend in my breadfruit tree will have the best view and not become nervous because he can't see us."

My heart rate spiked, and in a flash of panic, I froze, wondering if I should run for cover.

Ray said, "You're a dangerous man, Antonio. Some precautions make things safer."

"True, true, Mr. Jones. Now, please sit. We have a lot to discuss, and if we take too long, the fire ants will find your friend in my breadfruit tree."

I sat down on the painted wood bench and put my hands on the rough pealing tabletop, hoping that the small tremors in my hands would not be noticeable. My heart was still racing, but my panicked desire to run for cover was replaced by a feeling that my fear had somehow shown, and I had lost some respect in my host's eyes. Mendoza gave me another quick inspection that told me he had seen my brief panic and a slight twitch of his mouth told me it was what he had expected.

At that moment, I realized what I had seen in the pale eyes was not malice or danger but a deep, cold intelligence and planned calculation.

I took a few calming breaths while Ray and Mendoza moved around the table and sat. By the time we were all seated facing each other, I had recovered from the shock of Mendoza knowing about John, and I was able to calmly look the man in the eye and say, "Martin Shields told us that you are a major owner in the third tier of the company."

Mendoza smiled and then, in what seemed like a staged gesture, looked down at his hands. Looking at his hands, he said, "I respect both of you. I know you are both dangerous but good men, and I don't want any trouble from the two of you. I am as concerned and confused by the killing of my fellow owners at StreGo as you are." Slowly, he raised his head, and his eyes, which were nearly white in the afternoon sun, seemed to bore into me. "I am a small man; in my home, I had to work very hard to survive; if I thought I could become wealthy by killing the men and women of StreGo, I would not hesitate to do it."

He kept his calm, controlled eye contact on me for a long second, letting me absorb what he had just said. Then, in the same flat, calm voice, he continued. "That being said, I understand your suspicions about me, but I assure you I am not killing my partners. As good an idea as that might be, I must confess, I, in this case, am the hunted and not the hunter."

"You got the manpower," Ray said.

"I agree, and the motive." He said, turning his gaze to Ray.

"If I were you, I would be your prime candidate, but I'm not your man, " he said, raising his hands in an "it's that simple" gesture.

"Who is?" I asked.

When Mendoza turned his gaze back to me, there was a new element in his strange eyes, a sparkle that was the product of his shrinking pupils. "If I knew that, Mr. Cotton, he would be dead."

I felt a chill and knew without any doubt that I had just heard the stone-cold truth. As the cowboys on TV used to say, "No brag, just fact."

As we talked, a tall, slender black woman came out to the table and brought a pitcher of bush tea and three glasses of ice. I thought of John sitting in the breadfruit tree, his sniper rifle trained on us as we drank tea, and Cheri in the bush, hopefully still hidden. She must have been wondering what the hell was going on as we sat chatting like three friends at a Cruzan tea party.

"I know Mr. Ziggy made a wise decision when he hired you, and I know you will do your best to find out who this thug is who is killing my partners and probably hunting me. I have all my resources looking, but I have no idea who our mutual enemy is," he said to me between sips of the pungent bush tea.

For nearly an hour Mendoza shared his considerable knowledge and insight into the structure and people of StreGo. It was clear he had done his research. It was also clear although he understood there were a lot of possible suspects, he had no idea who the killer was.

Finally, Ray said, "The message you're sending is if we need help, you're there?"

Mendoza seemed to consider what Ray had said before he spoke, "In this, the three of us have a very serious mutual interest so yes, I and my people will be there. I have people in the VIPD and the government who are listening but not hearing. Should I learn anything I will share it with you."

"And you want us to share our information?" I asked.

"Your reports to Ziggy are enough, he sends everything you give him to me."

I was surprised that Ziggy was communicating with Mendoza but after I thought about it, the sharing of information made some sense.

We stood up and Ray asked," OK if I use your bathroom?"

"Sure," Mendoza said pointing toward the main house. "Maria," He yelled, "show my friend, Mr. Jones where the can is."

"Thanks," Ray said and headed toward the large house's doorway where the tall black woman that had brought our drinks stood.

# CHAPTER 24

When we were safe in my truck and driving back down the dirt road, Ray pulled off his wraparounds and gave me a shake of his head, "That, my friend, is one scary little mother fucker," he said.

I felt the pent-up tension and overdose of adrenaline flow out of my body and gave a nervous laugh, "When he mentioned John in HIS tree, I about shit."

"I noticed," Ray said with a big smile, "I thought you were gonna start shooting up the place right then and there."

We both laughed, and when the laughter died down, the mood in the truck became serious. "He's not our guy," I said.

"Nope."

"I think if he knows anything, he will tell us."

"If he can't fix it himself and needs our help, he will tell us," Ray said.

"Yeah," I agreed.

"You plant your bug?" I asked.

"Yeah, the couch in the front room should be a good spot."

There are a lot of people in this world that want to be bad and mean. In my experience, most of them are scared or just plain stupid, rather than dangerous. On a rare occasion, you will meet someone who is truly dangerous.

Not crazy, not full of false bravado, not felony stupid, but instead very smart, very sane, and very dangerous. In my career as a police detective and now a private detective, I have met only a handful of people I would consider truly dangerous; I was sitting next to one of them and driving away from another. I was sure that Antonio Mendoza had been genuine at our meeting and was as concerned with the systematic assassinations of the StreGo partners as we were. I also felt we had an ally, but a very dangerous ally. Ray's bug would be an asset in keeping our new best friend from becoming our worst nightmare.

"Can we trust him?" I asked more to myself than Ray.

Ray was looking forward and didn't turn to face me. I looked at him, and he seemed to be in his own world.

"Ray?" I said.

Slowly, he looked over at me and gave me a flat stare.

"What's up?" I asked, surprised by the concern on his face.

" You asked if we could trust him."

"Yeah," I said, turning my attention back to my driving.

Ray looked out the window and gave me a shake of his head before speaking, "I knew Antonio's father, Louis. It was a long time ago, and I was thinking of him. When I was in high school, Louis Mendoza ran the boys at Mutual Homes just like his son does now. He was gunned down right in front of little Antonio when Antonio was maybe eight. Antonio's mother was an amazing woman. After Louis died, she worked at Plaza Extra and raised Antonio alone. I used to see her when I would go shopping and always asked about little Antonio. She died when Antonio was 12 or maybe 13 in a botched robbery.

"Both parents?" I asked.

"I remember Antonio at his mother's funeral," Ray's voice seemed to trail off.

"And?"

Ray's attention seemed to snap back to me.

"And?" I repeated.

"And I got a real good idea who killed his father, his mother, the streets talk, and I listen," Ray said quietly, still gazing out the front window.

"And," I prompted.

"They're all dead," he said as if the idea was an afterthought.

"You're thinking, Antonio."

Ray's hands seemed to be moving as if he were counting. Then he spoke, "A bunch of the guys from Frederiksted got together one night and did a drive-by in Mutual Homes trying to kill a guy that had burnt them in a drug deal. There were two carloads of them, and they only managed to break a bunch of windows. Louis Mendoza was like the Godfather in Mutual Homes, which, considering he was a

Puerto Rican, was very unusual. Louis was related to about half the guys that had done the drive-by. He took the shooting real personally, and he and little Antonio went to a little gas station where most of the Fredericksted guys hung out. Long story short, a bunch of people went to the morgue that night, and Louis Mendoza, Antonio's father, was one of them.

"He took his son to a meeting like that?" I asked.

"Yeah," Ray said, "The rumor on the street was that the guys from Fredericksted started shooting when Louis pulled up, and he never even got to talk to them. Louis drove his car into the whole bunch of them and then got out blazing, but there were just too many. When the cops showed up, they found little Antonio huddled on the floorboard of the passenger's side of the car."

"Shit," I said, thinking about the impact something like that would have on a kid, especially a kid that had the IQ that Antonio Mendoza seemed to possess.

"The cops couldn't sort the whole mess out, and although a few of the Fredericksted guys were arrested, they were all released later."

"No one convicted of the drive-by or the killing of Antonio's dad?"

"Not a single one of those bastards got arrested. At the time, the Chief of Police was related to most of them. They just said self-defense and the whole thing was over," Ray said, beginning to count on his fingers again. "There were eleven guys at the gas station; Louis killed three of them;

the other eight have been killed or disappeared in the last ten years. Two are doing life in prison for other murders. One died of cancer about two years after Louis was killed. But the other five have disappeared since Antonio's mother died and are unsolved missing persons; one guy, a real delight named Polo, disappeared in Puerto Rico, and one in Miami was kidnapped for ransom, and even after they paid, he has never been seen again. The three others are all missing persons on St. Croix and presumed dead."

"Antonio?" I asked.

Ray turned to me and I saw a small nod in the dim light of the truck. "Yeah, when I look at it that way, Antonio."

Ray understands the underworld of St. Croix and the darker history of the island better than anyone I know and the look on his face in the dim truck lights was a realization, an understanding, of something that he had not considered.

"Five guys?" I asked, looking back at the road as we approached the stop sign marking the intersection with the main road.

Ray paused, moved his fingers some more, and smiled out toward the darkness. "Eight," he said, "There were three thugs from William's Delight involved in Antonio's mother's murder. They all were killed within two weeks of her shooting. Antonio was maybe twelve or thirteen at the time, so I never suspected him, but those five Fredricksted guys that dropped off the face of the earth all disappeared after Antonio's mother died.

"We're getting a little off track here, Ray," I said.

"Off track," Ray said a little surprised.

"Off track," I said, "We agree that Antonio is not our man, and so all this old history doesn't really matter to the case."

"Like it or not, Antonio Mendoza is a big part of this case, and I'm beginning to believe he may be a whole lot more dangerous than I originally thought."

"Those guys were all revenge if he even did it," I pointed out.

"Yeah," Ray said and continued in a Cruzan Chinese accent, "The man who does not know the history of his friends and enemies is foolish."

"Your new philosophy, Master," I asked, smiling at the unusual statement.

"Yes, my son," he replied as we pulled to the side of the road behind where John's big red truck was parked, and John and Cheri sat on the tailgate drinking beer.

Cheri had pulled on the black sweater she had chosen to wear and was in a white tee shirt and black BDUs. John was all smiles and still in his full camouflage.

"Nice camo," Ray said as he climbed out of the truck and accepted a cold, wet beer from John's cooler.

"Yeah, man, I was a ghost." John bragged.

"He knew you were there," I said with a smile toward Ray as I also took a beer, opened it, and took a long pull of the ice-cold liquid.

"What," John said, pulling the green cap off his head.

"Saw ya, you know, like saw ya," Ray said, poking John in the belly.

"Said you were in his tree like he owned it," I said.

"His tree," John said in a stunned voice.

"Yeah, Mr. Sneaky, he saw you," I said, pushing his big shoulder and giving him a big smile.

John looked at both of us and said, "No way."

"Yeah, way," Ray said, crushing the beer in his large hand and taking another out of the cooler.

"Shit." Cheri said, "If the shit had hit the fan, the big guy would have been a sitting duck."

"More like a sitting monkey," Ray said, patting John again.

"Sitting gorilla," I said, "monkeys are small and cute."

"I was so fucked," John said.

Cheri interrupted, "Hey if that's Mendoza's breadfruit tree, you think he'd let me pick some breadfruit?"

"I'll get you all the breadfruit you want, lady, if you promise not to go on that man's turf," Ray said.

"Good plan," I agreed.

"What's he like, think he may be our guy?" Cheri asked.

I looked at Ray, and he nodded, letting me know we were still sure about what we had learned. "Answer one," I said, "Mr. Mendoza is a very scary guy."

"Answer two, "Ray said, "He is not our guy."

"So much for the simple answer," she said with a shake of her head, "what now?"

John, who had been quiet since the revelation that he had been spotted, finally spoke up, "Maybe this was a bad idea."

"Nope," Ray said, patting the big man on the back.

"I think we got an ally, and I didn't like having a guy like Mendoza floating out on the edges of our investigation. Better to know as much as we can with a guy like that, "I said.

"He saw me," John said, crushing the can on his forehead.

"I haven't seen anyone do that since high school, "Cheri said with a shake of her head.

John smiled and tossed the empty can in the truck bed behind him.

"One good thing definitely came from this," I said. Ray got his bug in Mendoza's little clubhouse, so we should get word if there is anything going on, and we will know if Mendoza gets any leads on our killer."

"That's going to require we monitor the bug, and, trust me, that will be a pain in the ass," Cheri said, pulling another beer from the cooler.

"No worries," Ray said, "Cindy has the receiver and is taking turns with her sister monitoring the bug."

"I thought she was off island," I said, wondering if he had brought her back to help work on the case.

"Yeah," Ray said, "she is gone, but she can call me on my cell at any time, and I have the raw feed from the bug going into a direct link to her computer. There may be some breaks in the transmission because of communication breakdowns, but she can hear and record conversations from the playhouse most of the time. If she hears anything crucial, she calls me and we take it from there."

"Why didn't you tell us about that?" I asked.

"Just slipped my mind, but one thing we will need to clear is the data package I had to purchase for constant communication with the states was pricy, and I'll need the client to reimburse me."

"That shouldn't be a problem," Cheri said.

"Oh, I got the first text from her about 3 minutes ago"

"And," I prompted.

"I quote, '' Ray said as he looked down at his cell phone, "Ray, after you left, Mendoza came in and was talking to a woman; he said, "Those two are both crazy fuckers, but I think they're on our side." Ray shared a big smile. "Nice compliment I think."

I smiled, "I think Mr. Mendoza will be OK for now, and it appears he's not our guy."

# CHAPTER 25

Checking Mendoza off our suspect list was a good and bad thing. As I drove back to the boat with Cheri, I had a hard time figuring out the next move in the case. Finally, I looked over at Cheri, who was gazing out the passenger window.

"So," I said, "any ideas on where we go now?"

She turned to me and pulled out the list of the partners in StreGo that Martin Shields had given us. "Footwork and lots of interviews is all I can say."

"It's solved a lot of cases."

"Yep."

Cheri had no sooner spoken than her phone rang. She answered, and there was a long silence before she disconnected.

"That was Dory Hancock. Someone shot Ziggy," she said, her voice flat and her eyes beginning to well up.

"Dead?" I asked.

"No, he's at the hospital, shot him in the chest and missed all the vitals. Dory said he's in stable condition."

"Guards?" I asked.

"Dory said he will be watched twenty-four – seven."

"Should we go to the hospital?" I asked.

"No," Dory said, "not to come into the hospital. He has that end."

"Call Ray and John and let them know," I said as my mind began to race, trying to figure out an angle to get us to the killer before more people died.

While Cheri called Ray and John, I drove toward the boat. I was out of ideas, and I wanted to sit down with everyone and discuss our next move.

# CHAPTER 26

After being up most of the night before crawling around the bush outside Mendoza's compound, the stress of going into the compound for our meeting, and finding out about Ziggy's shooting, I was exhausted. By the time I had dinner, cleaned up, and paid some bills, I was totaled.

I turned off the lights in the salon and dropped down the steps into our stateroom. Cheri lay covered with a sheet, gently snoring, her glasses still on her face, and a book lying in her lap. I snuck up next to her, pulled off her glasses, and put the book on her nightstand. She gave a gentle grunt and rolled on her side. I had to smile. She had said, "Hurry down, I've got some ideas I want to share," when she had gone down into the stateroom.

I turned out the lights and laid down beside her in complete exhaustion. I was asleep in seconds.

The dream brought me wide awake. Like most dreams, most of it was gone, but I remembered the sight of Sam True, his body floating in his ritzy infinity pool, and the smell of his singed flesh. There was no chance of going back to sleep. The shock of the dream had left my heart racing and my mind churning.

I put my hands behind my head and tried to relax. Beside me, Cheri moved slightly and nuzzled against me. I began to try to catalog everything I knew about the case. First, my mind listed the known deaths of people associated with StreGo. The first had been StreGo's founder, Charlie Thomas. He had died in March, and his death had been ruled a heart attack. although he was young, nothing seemed odd about the death; I made a mental note to contact the coroner and see what had been on the toxicology screen. The coroner, Sally Matrix, was a good friend, and I was sure she would have no problem sharing the toxicology results.   I also had to talk to her about any chance of foul play causing the heart attack, but if there was nothing weird, I thought that I should rule Charlie Taylor's death as natural and not use it as a fact in the investigation.

Once Charlie was dead, any partner who was paying attention may have realized that their percentage of StreGo increased. I wondered what type of correspondence the company had sent out and if Charlie's death could have been the catalyst that stimulated the series of murders. Another mental note went into my list: get all correspondence between StreGo and its owners.

If Charlie had not been the victim of homicide but died naturally, that made Steve Whistler, who was run down in June, the killer's first real victim. I ran through my mind the things I knew about Whistler's death; Cheri had found out that he had been run over at the Sunshine Mall. He had been walking to his car late at night after finishing his shift at the movie theater where he worked as a manager. I made a mental note to ask Dory if he could get me the file on the hit-and-run. I thought about the hit-and-run and how it could be a planned killing or a spur-of-the-moment decision to act. Had the killer seen Whistler in the dark, deserted parking lot and made a rash decision to run him down? Had they spoken in the parking lot and maybe fought, resulting in the hit-and-run? I had no way of knowing, but on the long list of ways to kill people, a hit-and-run seemed more prone to a random act or a last-minute decision.

All I knew about the murder of Sue Fox was that she had died in August and what had been in the newspapers. The fire in her house had been an act of arson, but there were no facts about the actual method of the arson. I made a mental note to get the police investigation files from Dory and the arson report from the fire investigator. Could the killer's intent have been to scare Sue and ended in her death? I needed more facts.

Terry Jeffery, probably the third victim, had disappeared sometime in mid-September. If he was the third victim, his missing body was an anomaly in the case. No other victim's body had been hidden or disposed of. The fact that Terry Jeffery's was missing bothered me. I made a mental note to call Carl Rightner, a retired profiler for the FBI, and see if the disposing of a body and then not caring if bodies were found was a consistent pattern. I had to smile. For years as a homicide cop, I had believed profiling was a load of crap, and now I was calling Rightner for advice. I wondered what police files existed on Jeffery's disappearance and if an investigation of the disappearance might be a fresh direction for our investigation. I made a mental note to get the police files and see how complete they were. If the police investigation had holes or needed work, I might prioritize investigating the disappearance.

Martin Shields and his secretary had been the fourth and fifth victims, and they were pure and simple assassinations. There was no attempt to hide the killings, and the killer had relied on speed and a definite skill set to dispatch his victims. These killings were completely different from any of the other killings. Had a professional been hired? Had something snapped, and the killer decided just to start killing without any discretion. Was the killing getting easier? In some way, was the killer in some kind of transition? If so, the killer was becoming more dangerous. Also, the killing of Martin seemed less personal. Had it been planned, and was our meeting with Martin just a coincidence? Had the killer found out somehow, we had been hired, and that fact stimulated Martin's death. If our meeting with Martin had caused the killing of Martin and his secretary, how had the killer known so quickly about Ziggy hiring us and us having a meeting with Martin? I thought about the shot that had been taken at us from the hill and realized that the killer could have been on the hill watching when Ziggy had met with us at his gas station. If that were the case, the killer would have been on the hill twice, and I made a mental note to check houses on the roads that the killer could have used to leave his hiding place. I thought about what I knew about the area above the gas station. Tomorrow, I was going out to the gas station overlooking the hill and search for video cameras. It had been nearly two weeks since Martin's murder, so finding a private video camera with a two-week loop would be a long shot, but right now, I needed a lead.

One deadly clear thing was that the killer's actions were accelerating. In the last two weeks, he had killed Martin and his secretary, shot at the bar from the hill, killed Sam True and managed to shoot Ziggy.

I realized I didn't have any facts about Ziggy's shooting. Where had he been when he was shot? It also struck me that in the last two weeks, the killer had relied on guns except for the murder of Sam True. The murder of Sam True didn't seem to fit. It seemed personal in some way. I could imagine the killer watching the gas flow across the pool and the setting of the fire. The smell of the singed flesh that I had woken up with flowed like cancer into my mind, and my stomach took a small turn. It was time for a cup of coffee and a piece of toast. We had a long week in front of us, and it was time to get to work.

# CHAPTER 27

When Cheri came out of the stateroom, showered, and refreshed, I had just gotten off the phone with Dory and was on my second cup of coffee.

"Dory said Ziggy was shot by a high-powered rifle, probably a two-two three, and Cooper should have some ballistic comparisons later in the day, but it looks like the same person who shot at him when we were at the bar," I said in greetings

"My, you're a ball of sunshine," she said, pouring herself a cup of coffee and sitting beside me.

"Where was he shot?" she asked, taking a sip.

"His house."

"Any specifics, like where the shooter was or anything like that?"

"Nope, but Dory said he would meet us out there later today and fill us in. Right now, he's in a pissing match with his Captain to get assigned the shooting. Seems the big shots aren't ready to admit they have a serial killer on the island." I said.

"Big surprise, wouldn't want to fuck the tourist industry up any more than they already have," Cheri said, taking a piece of toast off my plate.

"So," she continued, "we meet with Dory sometime today. Do you have any other concrete plans?"

"Yeah," I said, outlining all the mental notes I had made while lying in bed that morning.

"Well, well, "she said with a smile, "your little brain is chipper this morning."

"Sleep, coffee, food, I'm a new man," I said, holding up my last piece of toast and giving her half.

She took my offering and said, "So what now?"

"I want to drive up on the hill in front of Ziggy's gas station and check out possible roads that the killer would have used to get in and out and see if there are any private video cameras that may have caught our killer driving in or out."

"Good idea, but most of those private videos are on twenty-four-hour loops." She said, "You want some bacon and eggs before we start this big day?"

## CHAPTER 28

In modern America, video cameras have changed the very fiber of police investigation. Along with the multiple government videos checking speed and intersections and securing government properties, there are also millions of private video cameras watching the actions of citizens. In the past, Ray, Cheri, and I spent hundreds of hours driving roads looking for "hidden" video cameras.

The hill in front of Ziggy's bar was a rabbit warren of small dirt roads. A smart killer, knowing that video would be used, would do their best to identify and not be seen by videos, but most killers aren't that smart. After two hours of looking, we had identified six possible video surveillance cameras. The trick now was to get the video footage as quickly as possible before it was automatically deleted. Ray got us our first good set of videos when he spotted a white video camera in front of a residence. When he approached the owner, the owner gladly took a full month of video off his computer and handed Ray a thumb drive packed with possible evidence. All we had to do was find the needle in the haystack.

By three o'clock, we had four possible videos that monitored three of the killer's possible roads into his shooting position. We decided to focus our search on the time we had been at the gas station for the first meeting, which was September 8th around three pm, and the time we had been shot at, which had taken place on September 11th around two pm.

Cheri also thought that a survey of all the tapes and logging cars going in and out should be done later, and Ray volunteered that Cindy could do that from where she was in the States if we sent her the data.

I was numb from viewing our first round of video when Dory called and arranged to meet us at Ziggy's house. Ziggy's house was a small ranch-style house that overlooked a perfect ocean view with the British Virgin Islands topping the horizon. Dory was in his unmarked patrol car when Ray, Cheri, and I pulled up the driveway and parked in the small dirt drive behind him. When Dory climbed out of his car, he had a banker's box and two three-ring binders.

" Got the files you wanted," he said in greeting, "and all hell will break loose if the brass finds out I shared this with you, so keep a lid on it, OK."

"Why are they fighting this so hard?" I asked, taking the box.

"Politics, Mad Dog, stupid ass politics. I don't know what happens to cop's brains when they get to the top of the hill, but they spend more time with their head in the sand than sniffing the breeze and trying to solve crimes. They drive me nuts."

"Some things never change," Cheri said, taking a brief look at the three-ring binders that were copies of Dory's murder books on the killing of Martin, his secretary, and Sam True.

"I got information from the detectives working on the other cases, but they won't give up their full investigative files. They think I might steal their cases and solve them, you know, make them look like the lazy assholes they are."

"You're in a bitter mood," Ray said.

"I was in meetings all day trying to convince the commissioner and chief that the killings are connected. It's like talking to a wall." Dory said with a frustrated head shake.

"Well, we've made a little headway," Cheri said, "Ray and Mad Dog met with Antonio Mendoza yesterday."

Dory smiled for the first time since he had gotten out of his cruiser, "You shitting me."

"Nope," Ray said, "nice guy."

"Yeah," Dory said, "like leprosy is a nice disease."

"We don't think he's our guy," I said.

"You guys overwhelmed by his denial of guilt or what," Dory said.

"No, First, Mr. Mendoza seemed to be genuinely concerned for his own well-being, but more importantly, since we left, he had three or four conversations telling his boys to figure out who's doing the killings," Ray said.

"Meeting," Dory said, and then his face went slack as he realized what we had done, "NO!" he said, and a huge smile grew on his face.

"Yep," Ray said, returning the smile.

"You got a bug on Antonio Mendoza?"

"Yep," Ray said, his voice rich with pride.

"Mendoza has his soldiers trying to solve this mess," Dory said.

"Yep."

Dory slammed his big hand down on the front of my truck and began to laugh.

"It's kinda nice on the dark side," Cheri said when Dory quit laughing, "and we never told you about the bug, right?"

Dory gave us all a big smile and said, "Even though this is the best news I've had in a week, I never heard a word." He then turned his attention to me and said nothing else, and I explained the video leads and how we were still checking the footage.

"If you have any trouble getting a video that may help, let me know, and I'll get you subpoenas."

"Some manpower to look at video wouldn't hurt," Cheri said.

"I'm it; VIPD has no manpower, sorry," he said, raising his hands.

"Anything you can get on the deaths of Fox and Whistler or the disappearance of Jeffery would be helpful," I said, thinking about the list of information that may help build our case.

"A lot of that is in the box, but not anything on the disappearance of Mr. Jeffery. The detective on missing persons is out on vacation but will be back tomorrow."

"Ok," Cheri said, "now that we've made your day, can you show us what you have here."

Dory walked through the estimated trajectory of the bullet and where he believed the shooter had set up, and we agreed to check out any possible video cameras that might have clues on them.

As Dory's cruiser dusted its way down the road, Ray said, "We got us some strange bedfellows."

# CHAPTER 29

After Dory left, we looked at the side of the hill the shooter had used as his hiding place.

"Lots of roads up there, you want to drive up and take a look?" Ray said.

"Yeah," I said, climbing into the truck.

The three of us drove for about thirty minutes before Cheri told us to stop at an overgrown old road on the far side of the hill that faced Ziggy's house. I got my machete, and we started walking up the hill. We had gone about eight feet, and Ray pointed out fresh footprints in the soft brown dirt. We walked around the tracks and were able to follow the trail up to the ridge of the hill. I stopped at the ridge and looked down. Ziggy's house and the spot where he had been shot were clearly visible about four hundred yards down the hill.

"Long ways, Mad Dog," Ray said as we began slowly combing the area. Thirty minutes later I spotted a flash of light just down the hill from the clearing on the rise of the hill. I took my machete and began to cut the thick growth between the shiny object and me. Before I got to the object I could see it was a shell casing. The casing had fallen down the hill and lodged on a small limb. I took out a pair of gloves from my pocket and a small plastic bag and began to reach for the shell casing.

"I wouldn't do that if I were you," Cheri said.

I looked back up the hill at her and asked, "Why not?"

"You take that shell casing and we become witnesses at a trial." She continued, "You know the standard bull shit that goes along with being a witness. Let Dory collect that shell casing."

"Ditto, Man," Ray said from behind me. "If it's evidence, let Dory take it."

"OK," I said tying the plastic bag to a branch so I could find the shell casing again. "Anything else."

"Dory will want forensics up here," Cheri said as she looked down the hill.

"We need to get video from the road leading to where you found the tracks up the hill," I said.

"I know the police have collected video from Martin's killing and in Gallow's Bay. I think we need to ask Dory for copies." Cheri said pulling out a small notebook she always carried and making a note.

"If you're getting video from all the crime scenes, don't forget Sam True and his neighbors; Choy is a closed community, and most of those people probably have video. My guess is the PD already has that video." Ray said.

"We catalog vehicles at each scene and look for cross over, but shouldn't Dory and VIPD be doing that kind of leg work?" I asked.

Cheri looked at me and shook her head, "That's the problem, Dog, they don't have the manpower to spend hundreds of hours looking at video."

"And we got an unlimited budget," Ray said.

I looked at Ray and Cheri, "Look, we can't even keep the people alive who are paying us, I'm a little worried about running up a big bill till we know we can get paid."

"Mr. Practical," Ray said, "Let's go talk to Ziggy and ask if we can spend a bunch of his money."

"We should probably go see him anyway," I agreed and we started back down toward our car.

# CHAPTER 30

When we got to his room, Mike Ziggler was slurping a milkshake and watching a rerun of Bonanza. He had a set of IVs in his arm and a set of monitoring patches on his bare chest. For a man who had been shot, he looked remarkably relaxed. He was sitting up, and when we entered his room, he greeted us with a large, if not somewhat goofy smile.

"Hi guy's" he said as we walked with Dory by the two-armed guards and entered his room. The four of us filled the small private room as we gathered around Ziggy's bed.

"You look chipper for a shooting victim," Cheri said coming over to Ziggy's bed and giving a peck on the cheek. "You are a lucky man, Ziggy."

"Tell me about it," he said, paling slightly. "The doctor said I fractured one rib and took eight stitches, so lucky is an understatement."

Ziggy's chest was bare, and I could see a large bandage on his side. "Feeling OK?" I asked.

"Mostly," Ziggy said, "This painkiller is good stuff." He gave a goofy smile again and lifted his left hand with a small black plunger at the end of a cord.

"Ah, painkillers," I said in a conspiratorial tone.

"If I could sell this stuff at the gas station, I wouldn't need StreGo, " he said as he pushed the plunger, and a soft "psst" sound emitted from his drug dispenser.

"Nice," Ray said.

In the last few years, we had both managed to get shot, and we both remembered the challenge of "if it hurts, just push this plunger."

"You up to talking?" I asked.

"Sure," he said, his eyes dulling slightly and his voice having a slight slur.

"Ziggy, we've spoken to quite a few of the partners and will continue to do interviews, but we want to look at another side of the investigation," I said, moving closer to Ziggy. I explained that we wanted his permission to hire someone to review the video.

As I explained, all I could think of was getting out of the hospital and returning outdoors. I hate hospitals, the smells of antiseptic combined with the constant chirping of monitors and the sanitarium green walls always manage to give me a headache.

Ziggy and the milkshake nodded.

"Between Dory's investigation and our investigation, we have gathered a bunch of video surveillance. We need to hire a few people to review all the videos and catalog them. With a little luck we may be able to ID a suspect or, at the very least, get some suspects to interview at or around the crime scenes."

Ziggy and the milkshake nodded again.

"Mr. Ziggler," Dory interrupted, "I would be glad to share copies of all the videos I have gathered during the investigation with Mad Dog. The problem is my department doesn't have the manpower to review these videos, and with Mad Dog and his people helping, we can get through this much faster."

"Lots of videos," Ziggy said, now more intent on the milkshake and Bonanza than our conversation.

"Maybe a hundred from different crime scenes," I said, looking at Dory, who had collected the videos for all the murder scenes.

Ziggy took the straw away from his mouth and pointed with the milkshake to the corner of the room. "Phone," he said, his speech slightly slurred. I heard the pump's "psst" sound. With a little luck, we could get authorization to go forward with the video reviews before Ziggy nodded off.

Ray grabbed the cell phone off the chair in the corner of the room and handed it to Ziggy.

Ten minutes later, we were out of the hospital and had full authorization to do the video reviews.

# CHAPTER 31

Tim Mason is a twenty-year-old computer whiz in his third year of study at the local junior college. Tim can take apart and rebuild a computer and is skilled in most software applications. I caught up with him at the University of the Virgin Islands computer lab.

Al Lester, a VIPD crime scene tech had recommended Tim. Al had spent a couple of semesters moonlighting as a computer science teacher and thought our best bet to find people to review tapes was at the college. He had said Tim Mason could put the little project together.

A student in the lunchroom led me to the lab and pointed Tim out. He was a large man who looked more like a football player than a computer geek. He stood an easy six-three and was athletically built with wide shoulders and powerful arms. He was wearing a Denver Bronco tee shirt that looked like it was painted on his powerful frame. As I approached him, he looked up at me with intelligent blue eyes and an easy, tooth-filled smile.

"Good morning, I'm Mad Dog Cotton, I think Al Lester might have called you and said I was coming over," I said.

Tim kept smiling as he rose from his computer. "Al said you have a project I may want to look at," he said.

"Did he say what it was about," I asked as we shook hands.

"Just that you may need some video reviewed."

"A lot of videos,"

"Have you got it with you?" he asked.

"Yeah," I said. "The video my people collected is in my truck, and the video the PD collected is being bought over by Detective Lester. He should be here in about ten minutes."

Tim reached down to the keyboard and entered a series of commands and the screen went blank. "How about you show me the video you got while we wait for Al."

Two hours later, I watched in stunned silence. After seeing the box of videos Al had brought over Al and I calculated we had a total of eighty-two videos. Al and the VIPD forensic team had collected sixty of the videos. Each of the VIPD videos was in a clear evidence bag. Each bag for the VIPD was marked in black marker with the date, time, and where it had been retrieved. Each bag also had the name of the officer who had collected the evidence and a chain of custody that showed that Al had taken the videos from the evidence locker and taken possession of the videos.

My twenty-two videos were in manila envelopes and marked with time, date, location, and either Ray, Cheri, or my name. Al took each of my videos and signed them into an evidence sheet. He then took each manila envelope and its contents and put them into a clear VIPD evidence bag.

"Mad Dog," he explained, "I am now taking custody of your videos. You OK with that?"

"Sure," I said.

It took us about an hour to enter all of my evidence into VIPD's evidence bags and complete all the paperwork. When we had signed the last transfer sheet and filled out the evidence bag, Al and I went to find Tim.

# CHAPTER 32

Tim had gotten permission to work on the project from the computer science department and set up a computer lab in one of the small empty offices in a deserted hallway of the oldest wing of the college. When we found him, to my amazement, he was surrounded by five computers from the computer science department. The five computers were now arranged in a circle of wires and miscellaneous equipment around the room, and Tim sat in the middle of the wild mess on a rolling chair, going from computer to computer.

"OK, Tim," Al said as we entered the room, "we've got the video marked as evidence and ready for me to sign it over to you."

Tim looked up from a computer he was hooking up and came over to look at the two boxes of evidence bags we were carrying. "Are you going to stay or sign the video over to me?"

"I'll stay as long as I can, but I think that we should go through the formality of signing the videos over to you," Al said.

As I sat at an empty table watching, Al and Tim filled out the necessary documents and made notations on each of the clear evidence bags that formed the chain of custody from Al to Tim. Al's cell phone rang when the last bag of evidence was processed.

Al went to the far side of the room and returned in a few minutes, "Sorry guys," he said, "I gotta run. We got a homicide out at the Kennedy Projects." Without another word, Al left. I stood at the door of the computer lab that Tim had just assembled and listened to Al's footsteps as he walked down the empty corridor of the vacant wing of the college and departed the building with a slam of the door at the end of the hall.

I looked around the chaotic room and thought that the empty halls and the dark, vacant wing of the building gave me the creeps.

"OK, Mad Dog," Tim said, returning my wandering mind to business. These videos are in multiple formats. The first thing I need to do is get all the videos in one single format, which is tricky because no software will allow me to reformat all the videos.

I shook my head and stayed silent.

"OK," Tim said, picking up a video cassette. "This video cassette, let's say, is video type A."

I again just shook my head.

"The only way to watch this video and understand what is on it is to simply watch it. We have about 30 videos like this that were collected," He explained.

"We better get to watching," I said, ready for a long boring night.

"No watching, Mad Dog," he said with an easy smile. "If you and I just watched this video and cataloged everything we saw, we would be here for weeks."

"That's why I make the big bucks," I thought.

"We're going to let the computer do most of the watching." He said.

"I don't understand." I said, "We're not watching these videos tonight?"

"Nope," he said, giving me his easy smile. First, we'll take all the cassette videos and put them in digital format that I can work with to run recognition software to see if the same cars or persons show up on different videos."

"Digital format?" I asked, feeling increasingly intimidated by the incomprehensible ball of wires, screens, and hardware set on the five tables surrounding us.

Tim gestured with the black cassette in one of Al's clear evidence bags and pointed at one of the flash drives. "That video on the flash drive is in a different digital format,"

I gave Tim my best, "I don't get it look" and he gave me his best, "don't worry," look.

"I'll tell you what, Mad Dog, I've got this end of the deal. I don't think there's much you can do to help, so if you want to work on your investigation, I will bang away at this and call you and Al if I get something."

"You sure?" I asked.

"Yep," he said with a smile as he ushered me out of the bright light of the computer lab and into the half-light of the long hall outside the lab. The empty hall was only lit by the light flowing from the lab and the light shining through the glass doors about fifty yards ahead of me. As I walked, I could hear each of my steps echo in the emptiness. Behind me, I heard the rollers of Tim's chair as he rolled from computer to computer, getting ready to do whatever it was he would do to the videos. I could smell the faint hint of mold that brought back memories of empty, dangerous halls from my past. I hurried my steps toward the light of the glass doors at the end of the hall.

# CHAPTER 33

From the college parking lot, I watched the sunset over tall trees that lined the college's campus. As I watched the high wispy clouds above me turn a deep burning orange, the chill I had felt walking the empty college halls melted away. My mind was racing. I didn't know how long Tim would take to review the tapes and felt like I should have stayed and reviewed tapes the old-fashioned way as he worked, but it had been clear that Tim knew what he was doing, and I was in the way.

The case was beginning to wear on my nerves; we had been working for seven days and making huge money, but I was ashamed to say that we had made no progress. The killer or killers were moving along nicely, killing off StreGo owners at a rate of about four a week. At the rate the killings were taking place, we would be out of investors and suspects soon. I had the awful thought of more killings, and my stomach turned. I had worked on serial killer cases before and knew these were nearly impossible cases. The more a man kills, the better they get, and all the investigator can do is wait for a mistake. Leg work like interviews and Tim's review of the video was effective, but unlike the TV shows where computers, hair, and DNA track down the killer, the real-life fact was if they didn't make a big mistake, serial killers are damn hard to catch. "Get back to work, Cotton," I said aloud and made my next move forward. I called Ray.

"What!" Ray asked in an angry voice as he answered.

"Howdy, grumpy," I said in a happy voice I didn't feel.

"Mad Dog, that you?" he asked.

"No, it's the good fairy," I answered, "what's got you so pissy?"

"I have been trying to call your dumb ass for an hour, and all I get is your messages. What the fuck!"

I hit the speaker on my phone's screen and looked at the side of my phone. My phone was in what Cheri calls the no-call mode.

"Sorry, man, I must have bumped the no-call button on the side of my phone." I said, moving the little button back"

"Cheri and I have been looking at a new stiff for an hour."

I thought of Al and the call that took him to the Kennedy Projects. "Kennedy?" I asked.

"Yeah, how do you know that?"

"Long story," I said, "now fill me in."

"Bobby D. Wilson shot once in the head with a small caliber handgun. Up close and personal, same as Martin and his secretary."

"Damn," I said as I started my truck and drove out of the college parking lot. "Any witnesses?"

"Fuck no, since when do we get that lucky," Ray said, and then he must have handed the phone to Cheri.

"Where the fuck have you been?" she demanded.

"At the college getting the tapes reviewed., that little button on the side of the phone must have got moved."

"You and that damn phone. Mad Dog, you will have to learn how to run that thing."

"I was beginning to worry…" I heard a touch of fear in her voice.

As I pulled the truck onto Queen Mary Highway, I started racing toward the Kennedy project. "I'm sorry," I said again.

"Fuck it," she snapped. "Just get down here and bring the video recorder. I want to video this crowd. The killer may be watching this mess, and I want a record." The phone shut off.

I guess I was in trouble again. Oh well, some things never change.

# CHAPTER 34

I parked in the Pueblo grocery store lot and walked across the street and down into the crowd that had gathered on the Kennedy Housing Project's common lawn. The crowd seemed to mostly consist of residents who had come out to watch the police as they tried to work the crime scene and interview possible victims.

I worked my way through the crowd till I saw Ray standing a head taller than everyone around him. I waved and he walked toward me.

"Cheri still pissed?" I asked as the crowd parted and Ray reached me.

"Man, for some reason, when she couldn't reach you, it spooked her. I guess too many people dying around us." He said as he turned and headed deeper into the crowd.

I caught up to Ray and said, "I don't remember Wilson on the list. Why are we here?"

"I haven't been able to talk to Dory. He's in one of the small cinder block houses at the end of the road with a witness. All I know is he called Cheri when he couldn't get ahold of you and told her we had another victim tied to StreGo.

We came around one of the large project apartment buildings and I could see a ring of police cars and a clump of blue uniforms. Al Lester's forensic van was parked by the TanTan bushes that formed the border of the housing project. Since Dory was busy, I walked over to see what Al was working on. I saw Al and he waved me over.

The last hints of light were fading and the barrier of thick bush looked dense and ominous as I approached Al. He was scanning the bush with a large flashlight.

"Killer came out of the bush here," Al said pointing at a single footprint in the damp soil at the edge of the thick brush. There's a trail here that goes up to the Chinese joint at the top of the hill. He pointed up the hill with the light.

"Not everyone knows that. "I said.

"Nope." Ray said, "only people know about this trail will be locals or cops, guys who are not familiar with this would never go into the bush and just find a trail."

"Why cops," I asked.

"We know it," Al said, "we do about a crime a week here and this trail is a favorite bolt hole for the bad boys."

I nodded and asked Al, "How's this tie to the StreGo case?"

"Don't know," Al said and pointed back to the cinder block duplex, "Dory has got a witness in that building. You might walk up and see if he will talk to ya."

"Anything here?" I asked.

"Sure, one foot print I can cast." Al said.

I thanked Al and Ray and I walked up to the pink cinder block house where Dory had his witness. Cheri was standing against the wall of the building when I got there talking on the phone. She gave me a shake of her head that said, "this is getting crazy," and went back to talking on the phone. Ray and I walked to the closed door and knocked.

Dory opened the door, saw me, and came out.

"I hear you got a witness," I said as he stepped out of the small duplex.

"Not an eye witness, but a witness that ties this case to the others."

"How?" Ray asked.

"The gal inside was Wilson's girlfriend. It seems he was over at Gallows Bay when the shooting there took place. Instead of coming to us with an ID of the killer, he tried to shake the killer down. Had the girl friend write a letter to the killer saying he wanted ten grand or he would go to the cops."

"That didn't work so good," Ray said shaking his head.

"Nope," Dory said with a slight smile, "I'd say it kinda back fired."

"I wonder how many other witnesses are out there that aren't talking." Ray said.

Dory just shrugged his big shoulders.

"Plenty of video cameras up at the top of the hill," Ray said, "Want us to gather them up?"

"I already have three detectives up talking to people and getting video, we're cool but if you got some cash, I think a bounty might be worthwhile. We gotta slow this guy down, five shootings in a week is crazy."

"I think we may be able to arrange a nice bounty," I told Dory. "Will the Chief and Commissioners be OK with it?"

"Already cleared, the assholes won't declare this a serial killer so we can get help from the feds, but I did talk them into a bounty as long as the territory isn't out any cash." Dory said. "I'll have Al take the video to Mason as soon as they have it all gathered and logged into evidence. How are things going at the college?" he asked me.

"Great," I said, "That kid seems to be hard at it, I don't really understand what he's doing but it may be our best lead."

Like he had been listening and waiting for an intro my phone rang. It was Tim Mason. I listened and then mouthed, "Mason" to Dory, Cheri, and Ray, "he says he's got something."

"You three go, no reason to be here," Dory said, "and let me know what the kid's got."

# CHAPTER 35

The college wing where Tim's computer lab was set up was dark when we entered but you could see the light of the lab on at the end of the hall. Tim must have heard us coming because he met us at the door to the lab.

In the luminescence of the florescent light, his white teeth gleamed as he smiled and said, "Got you guys some good stuff,"

"Talk," I said.

"I'm only about five percent through the video but I think I already have a good lead," he said as he led the three of us to the center of the room.

When we were in the center of the five monitors and could see all five, Tim began to speak. "I have these four computers reformatting video and that is slow going but there were five videos in the format I was able to run through my recognition software in their original format. They are of the roads above Ziggy's on the day you were shot at, three videos of the parking lots by Mr. Shield's office at the time of his killing and finally a video from the street where Sue Fox was killed in the arson of her house. In those three groups of videos, I identified one possible vehicle that was present in each set of videos."

Tim stopped talking and worked on the keyboard of one of the computers for a second and a grainy black and white photo of a truck appeared. "This truck was at all three locations."

"Pay dirt," Ray said, looking at the photo.

"Are you sure? There are a lot of white trucks on this rock." Cheri said.

Tim sat down at a computer that showed the grainy white truck and typed out a series of commands. The screen split into five screens, each showing a white truck.

"In these photos, you look for anomalies in the trucks, scratches, dents, types of wheels, etc. When I identify a certain anomaly, I have the computer use its recognition software to look for similar trucks with similar anomalies. A red circle on the screen highlighted a dent on the rear corner of the truck.

"See this dent," Tim smiled at the screen and pointed.

Cheri shook her head, and he continued, "This dent has about a hundred digital points of identification based on identifiers like size, placement of rust, and location on the truck."

"OK," Cheri said.

"All I have to do is tell the computer to find matches to the dent in other photos, and because that part of the truck is random, the computer can quickly scan all the video just for that very specific set of pixels or pattern of pixels in photos. When I search, my program will allow me to find probable matches which don' require the exact angle, lighting, and other variables. The FBI technicians that do this type of recognitions recommend a seventy-five percent match for searching and ten points of identification for what they consider a valid match; they go on to recommend a twelve-point match for court."

"Points of identification like in a fingerprint?" I asked.

"Exactly," Tim said, "The idea is based on a mathematical probability model that a guy named Gatlin formulated to quantify how accurate fingerprints were in identifying an individual. In a nutshell, twelve points of identification are considered pretty much a bulletproof match. Men have been sent to death row based on seven points of identification."

"So, you take this dent and look for it on the video?" Ray said, pointing at the rear panel of the white truck.

"Basically yes," Tim answered, "basically once I identify an anomaly that is unique, like the dent in this truck, I can tell the computer to analyze that specific set of photographic pixels and find likely matches. I do a more complete analysis when I find a likely match."

"I trust you, Kid," Ray said, his attention fixed on the truck. " Bottom line."

"This truck was at all three locations, one hundred percent probability," Tim said.

"Got plates," Ray said.

"Not yet, but I have about a hundred more videos that will show different angles of the truck, and by the time I'm done, I can send you out of here looking for an exact truck."

"How long will it take to get through all the video?" I asked.

"The recognition software just looking for this dent can go through a thirty-minute video in forty seconds with my equipment. The problem is reformatting this video. The videos you brought me are in about six different formats. I don't have the software or hardware to reformat some of the videos from some of the older videos, and the stuff I am reformatting is somewhat slow."

Tim pointed at one of the four screens that seemed to be scrolling numbers. "This video will be done in about five minutes. It's from the mall's video loop and has a good chance of capturing Steve Whistler's hit-and-run suspect driving in the parking lot outside the theater. Al thought it should be one of the first videos I reformatted. If you guys want to wait, in about ten minutes, I can have it run through the recognition software, and we may know more."

"I'll go across the street and buy beer," Ray said.

"Cokes, Ray," Cheri said, "I could hear the defense attorney now, "and Mr. Mason, isn't it true that when you working with the evidence, you and the people you were with were drunk on your asses?" bring Coke."

"Shit, you're no fun," Ray said as he turned and walked out the door.

Right after Ray left, the screen reformatting the theater video announced it was complete, and Tim took out a flash drive and transferred the completed video to the computer with the white truck on its screen. The screen went blank, and then a video of the theater's parking lot appeared. The video started displaying in very fast motion and, in a matter of seconds, announced, "Match found" in a metallic voice.

"Bingo," Cheri said as a white truck with a clear dent on its right rear corner panel appeared.

"That's your truck," Tim said, working the keys, "now, let's see if we get lucky."

Tim punched some keys, and the truck began to move in the video. It was driving down the length of the parking lot with its driver side exposed. At the end of the lot, it turned and disappeared behind a row of shrubs."

"No such luck," I said, "I was hoping for a license."

"Patience," Tim said, and we continued to watch the screen. A minute later, the truck appeared at the end of the parking lot, getting ready to pull into traffic. Tim stopped the video and began to type on the keyboard, and the image of the truck grew.

"Close enough for a license plate?" Cheri asked.

"Maybe," Tim said in a whisper. Seconds later, the black and white grainy license appeared.

"It looks like FISH M," Cheri said as Tim adjusted the video."

"It is FISH M," I said, "We got an ID.

Tim raised his hand, and we both gave him a high five.

"What's the deal," Ray said, standing at the door holding five Cokes."

"Pop those tops, Ray," I said, feeling the first real joy since the case started, "It's time to celebrate we got FISH M."

# CHAPTER 36

"I'm telling ya, Cotton, there is no FISH M license in the system," Dory said, his voice angry.

"There has to be," I said.

"No, not a fucking thing."

"OK, Dory, you still need to put out an all-points bulletin and have every cop in St. Croix looking for a white truck with a FISH M license. I'll also have Tim send over photos of the truck so the officers can look for it. The truck has a specific dent in the rear corner panel."

Dory agreed to put out an all-points bulletin on the truck and thanked us. I put the phone down. It had been a crazy thirty minutes, and our mood had gone from the high of discovery to this low. I felt punched in the gut.

"Don't worry, be happy," Tim said in a calm, cheerful voice.

"What," I said.

"I said, Mad Dog, 'don't worry, be happy,' I'm just getting started, you go home and, in the morning, come back, I'll have a lot more."

Ray crushed his empty Coke can and said, "Fuck it, man, win a few and lose a few. I'm going to go get some sleep."

As we walked down the dark corridor leading from the makeshift computer lab to the college entrance, Cheri stopped and said, "Wait."

While Ray and I stood in the dank, dark hallway, Cheri quickly walked back to the computer lab. We waited for about five minutes before Cheri came back down the hall.

"What was that all about," I asked as she got back to us.

"A hunch,"

"Want to share," Ray said as we turned and followed Cheri toward the college exit.

"I had Tim blow up the tag on the license. The FISH M plate was from 1993."

"That vehicle hadn't been licensed since 93?" I asked.

"Or," she said, "the killer is using an old plate."

"Whose old plate," I asked.

"Let's call Dory and see if he can find out," Cheri said.

We dropped Ray off at his vehicle and continued to the boat. On the way, Cheri left a detailed message for Dory.

After three days with only a few hours of sleep, I was asleep in a matter of seconds after sliding between the sheets.

# CHAPTER 37

The sirens wailed from somewhere in the dark. The smell of burned flesh and gasoline filled my senses, and my eyes watered from the black smoke that rolled up from the hole. Out of the darkness of the hole, a scream for help and a cry of terror rose. The taste of bile rose from my throat as I realized the person in the black smoke-filled hole was Cheri. With a scream of anger and fear, I ran and jumped into the swirling black smoke. I was falling, falling, and the screams had stopped. Cheri no longer screamed. I realized I had quit screaming. The smell of burning flesh engulfed me and I heard a distant laughter. The laughter built, and suddenly, in a panic, I realized I was on fire! I wanted to roll, but I was still falling. I hammered my hands against the flames and began to scream.

Then I heard the voice, I knew that voice, "Mad Dog" it screamed "Mad Dog, wake up." My eyes slammed open, and the dark stateroom came into focus.

"You're OK, Dog, you're OK!"

I looked up into Cheri's worried eyes. "Shit," was all I could say. The nightmare was still hammered into my mind.

After a short time, Cheri went back to sleep, and I lay awake, my mind still stuck on the vivid memory of the nightmare. I couldn't shake the fact that I was missing something, a fact that my subconscious had known. Thought nagged at me that something in the nightmare was important. I listened to Cheri's soft breathing and the night sounds of the boat. I let my mind drift away from the nightmare and concentrate on the soft lapping of the water against the boat, the faint howl of a light wind through the rigging of the sailboats. Far away, a car started, and I heard the faint purr of an engine as it drove from the parking lot above the docks.

I considered getting up and going up to the salon, but the bed felt warm and comfortable. I rolled over and laid my hand against Cheri. It was just a touch, just a reassurance that all was well.

## CHAPTER 38

It was 8:30 when my phone rang. I was still in a deep sleep, and it took me a second to groggily answer.

"Yeah," I was able to grunt, trying to make the jump from sleep to awake.

"Mad Dog, it's Al Lester," the phone said, and my half-conscious mind struggled to understand.

"Al?" I said.

"We got a problem," the voice said.

I forced myself to sit up and said, "Just a minute." I shook Cheri, who was curled up next to me, and as she woke, I put my phone on speaker. "Ok, Al," I said as Cheri rolled over and slid up to a sitting position.

"We got a problem," Al repeated.

"Yeah, you said that," I replied, "What?"

"I went to the lab this morning to see how Tim was coming and someone has torched it."

My mind snapped to full consciousness. "What?" I said.

"I got here, and there's an army of fire trucks. I can see the window to the lab, and smoke is rolling out of it."

"Is Tim OK?" I asked.

"I don't know," Al said, "I just got here."

"I'll be there," I said, "Call Dory."

"OK," Al said and hung up.

"Shit," Cheri said as she climbed out of bed and slipped into a pair of shorts.

I called Ray.

The small parking lot outside the college wing where the computer lab had been was full of emergency vehicles when we pulled up.

Ray was sitting next to his big white SUV, drinking a cup of coffee, and motioned to the parking space next to his vehicle. I swung my truck in and parked.

Cheri was out of the truck before I had the truck in park, barking at Ray, "Tim, is Tim OK?"

Ray raised his big hands and shrugged his shoulders. "Sorry, Cheri, I just pulled in and was waiting for you guys before I go over." He looked over his shoulders at the pandemonium caused by the dozens of uniformed men standing outside the entrance to the college.

I spotted Dory and Al coming across the lot toward us in a fast walk.

Cheri moved toward them and yelled, "Tim?"

"We don't know yet," Dory said as he reached us. "The firemen are still in the lab going through the wreckage."

"Have you tried to call him?" I asked.

"Yeah," Al said, "I got a message."

"I'm going to go back over and see what I can find out, "Dory said.

At that time, an ancient wreck of a red jeep pulled up to the knot of fire trucks, and Tim leaped out. I saw a fireman restrain him, and two uniformed officers had to hold the young man back.

"Thank god," Cheri said as the four of us rushed across the parking lot to where Tim was still struggling with the two uniformed officers.

Dory stepped between the officers and Tim and, in a firm voice, said, "I got this,"

The officers backed away as Dory tried to calm a frantic Tim.

"What the hell," Tim gasped, "Look at my lab, what the hell."

Cheri pushed by Dory and gave Tim a tearful hug.

"What?" Tim stammered as Cheri released him.

"We thought, "she said, and she motioned at the still-smoldering building.

"Oh," Tim said, and his deep, tanned face blanched to a pale white. "Oh shit."

"But you're OK," she said, taking his head and holding his pale face.

"Where the fuck were you, man?" Ray asked, "We thought you were in there."

"I took a break about four o'clock and ran home for a nap and a quick shower," he said.

"Shit, man, the tapes, all the tapes were in there." Ray said, "We're fucked."

I looked at the wisp of black smoke lifting out of the broken lab window and knew Ray was right. The tapes were our best lead, and they were destroyed in the fire.

"No way," Tim said, pulling a cigarette-sized silver box out of his front pocket. "I am a serious geek, man. I never let my data alone. I have got all the videos on this. It was the first thing I did when we got the video."

"You made a copy," Al said.

"Hell yeah," Tim said with a smile, "you never know when some whack job is going to burn down your lab."

The young man looked at the burned building and then back at Al. "What do you think, Professor Lester? The college is going to be pretty pissed."

Ray and Cheri began to laugh, and soon, we were all laughing. I noticed two soot-covered firemen watching us suspiciously, so I forced myself to quit laughing and give the two firemen a wave. They shook their heads and turned back to the building.

"We need to set up a new lab," Cheri said, "one that is safe."

"Any ideas," I asked.

"Yeah, man," Ray said with a smile, "I have an idea, and I have a little favor to call in."

# CHAPTER 39

The property Ray led us to overlooked the south-eastern shore of the island. We pulled up to the gate, and Ray made a call on his cell phone. The gate opened, and our little caravan pulled into the compound. We drove through the narrow road winding up a large hill until the road opened into the large open front of a towering home of glass and native stone.

"Wow," Cheri said, looking back at the view that captured most of the southern coast of St. Croix from the refinery to the far east end.

"Cool," Tim said from behind me.

"Welcome to your new lab," Ray said, looking back at Tim. This place was built by one of the Rockefellers when St. Croix was the stopping place of the rich and famous."

"How," Cheri said, looking at Ray.

Ray shrugged and said, "Don't ask; just be glad we have a place to hide out until this thing is over."

"No one knows?" I asked.

"I didn't even let Dory know," Ray said. "It's only Tim and us," Ray said, opening the door to his SUV.

The back of the SUV was stacked with food, computer equipment, and suitcases.

I grabbed some cases of water and followed Ray to the large mahogany front doors. Ray opened the door and let us in. We walked into a huge, great room. The great room was basically round and soared thirty feet above us in a series of tree-sized mahogany beams coming to a point at the top like a giant Native American Tee Pee.

The floors were tile, and our steps echoed as we walked across the expanse of the huge room. The far wall of the great room was a towering atrium overgrown with houseplants, dominated by a thirty-foot waterfall that flowed into a lily pad-covered pool.

"This is pure James Bond," Tim said as he entered, dragging his blue suitcase and black duffel bag.

"Hello," I said loudly, listening to the hollow echo as the sound bounced through the empty room.

"Can we set the lab up here?" Tim asked, setting down the bags and raising his head toward the lofty ceilings like a child who had discovered Wonderland.

"Cool with me," Ray said.

In two hours, we were settled in. Tim had five desktop computers again arranged in a circle around him. The great room seemed to dwarf the circle of light formed by the computers, and the late day streamed through the floor-to-ceiling windows and the massive skylights that helped form the cathedral-like ceiling.

Ray was comfortably sitting in a white leather sofa chair, probably napping, but his wrap-around mirrored sunglasses hid the truth.

Cheri and I had wondered into the kitchen area and were fixing sandwiches for the four of us when Cheri said, "We're going to want to get back out on the street and start interviews again, I think we should bring John in to keep an eye on this place."

"I'm good with that," I said. Also, if Ziggy is game, we should bring him up. He either needs to get off the island or we need to get him where he's safe, and this is as good as I think you can do."

Cheri nodded. "Did you have that talk with Tim about how long all this will take?"

"No, but I think we should ask him."

I loaded the sandwiches on a platter and set them on the twenty-foot granite countertop that divided the great room from the kitchen. "Come eat," I yelled, and Tim and Ray responded immediately.

I let everyone get a handful of ham and cheese sandwiches before I said, "Tim, we need an idea of how long the computer work will take."

Tim chewed thoughtfully on his sandwich and then, swallowing, said, "The truck recognition will be done by tomorrow. I'm still putting all the videos in a workable format, but that will be done by tonight. When the formatting is done, I need to get good recognition identifiers into the computer on the passenger side of the truck and the front and rear of the truck, which means I'll have to run each side of the truck through the recognition program. That will give me a much better idea of the presence of the truck and allow the computer recognition program to ID the truck no matter what angle we are looking at.

Once we have good, reliable identifiers, I will run the other crime scene video.

Another aspect that will take more time is that Al has given me access to the island's operational surveillance system that VIPD monitors. It consists of forty-two video cameras set up around the island. Once I have that surveillance and the identifiers for the four sides of the truck, I may be able to track the truck's movements right back to the killer's home. Also, I may be able to track those forty-two cameras live and see if we can find the truck on a live feed."

"Man can't hide these days," Ray said, shaking his head.

"You got enough computer power for all that?" I asked.

Tim nodded.

"I could use two more computers for another program I have been thinking about that might help. The truck's windows are tinted, so you can't clearly see the driver, but I can run software over select photos pulled from the video that will allow me to build a composite and maybe get an idea of the killer's identity."

"How?" I asked between chews.

"Well, when I get a good look at the driver's side window or the front window, I get mainly the black reflection of the tint, but some pixel characteristics are identifiable of the driver by taking hundreds or thousands of these little pixel clues, I think I may be able to reconstruct the drivers face. It won't be exact, but at least it will give us a hint. You know, male, female, some facial features, hair length, stuff like that."

"How long?" I asked excited by the thought of an ID of the ghost that had been hunting down the StreGo owners.

"It's hypothetical, but I should be able to cobble various software programs and basically design a hybrid program to pull the face out of the tinted darkness. It may go fast or never work. I just don't know."

"Video ID is the best use of time now," Ray said, standing and moving to the fridge. "Right."

Tim raised his hand and gave Ray a one-finger signal, and Ray tossed him a can of Miller Lite.

Ray came back with three more beers, and we all popped the caps.

Ray raised his beer and looked at Tim. "It seems to me we got us a fourth Musketeer in our little group." He said.

"Fifth," Cheri said, "Let's not forget Big John."

"Five it is," Ray said, clinking our beer cans together, "To the five Musketeers of St. Croix."

"Speaking of John, where is he?" I asked.

"He said if he was going to play bodyguard, he had to pick up some toys," Cheri said.

"I like John's toys," Ray said with a smile.

"I talked to Dory, and he's agreed to turn Ziggy over to us as soon as the hospital releases him," I said.

"He's not getting off the island?" Tim asked, concern in his voice.

"No, he wants to stay," I said.

"Fucking stupid, "Cheri said.

"Man, got to do what he gotta do. Mr. Ziggy wants to see this through. I'm cool with that." Ray said.

"Still fucking stupid, "Cheri repeated.

"Hell, Cheri," Ray said, crushing the beer in his big paw and raising to get another, "life's stupid."

# CHAPTER 40

It was ten o'clock when the truck lights of John's truck topped the hill and spread rays of light into the upper part of the great room. Cheri pulled her Glock and moved Tim back into a center bedroom we had designated as the "safe room" while Ray and I went out and met with John. Big John jumped down from the cab of his jacked-up truck cab and met us with a big smile.

"This is a hard son of a bitch to find," he said, looking at the glass and rock mansion.

"Hear you got toys?" Ray said, crossing the gravel drive and greeting John with a bear hug.

"Yeah, man," he said pointing to a box in the back of the truck, "and monitors, nobody coming to this party without an invitation."

"Can you have everything up and running by ten tomorrow morning?" I asked.

"Yep," he said, "I'll get started at first light and should be done in about two hours."

John grabbed the box and carried the equipment into the house. The plan was to have John guard Tim and Ziggy while Ray, Cheri, and I conducted more interviews.

The phone call came just as we got back into the house. I answered my cell and Dory said, "I had a clerk go back into the archives that plate was issued to a Mike Jones."

"Thanks for going to the trouble," I said, "that doesn't ring a bell, how about you,"

Dory's voice came back, "No."

"What's your game plan tomorrow?" I asked.

"Just left a shooting out at the Plaza West. It looks like I'm going to be working on it tomorrow. You're on your own, working the StreGo case. How's the kid doing with the videos?"

"Good," I said.

"I got authorization from Ziggy to have a five-thousand-dollar reward for information on Ziggy's shooting. That may break something loose."

"More likely a slew of crazies," I said.

"True," Dory said.

# CHAPTER 41

The killer felt invigorated for the first time since botching the hit on Ziggler.

A six-foot wave blasted over the bow of the Cigarette boat, and the spray of the ocean washed over the killer. The two huge engines on the back of the forty-foot speed boat roared, and the killer's mind danced to the rhythm of the slamming waves and the engine roar. The killer felt alive, powerful, invincible. The plan was coming together. The kills were lining up. The idiots at VIPD were chasing their tails, and the detectives Ziggler had hired were clueless.

In a moment of pure power, the killer roared a primal war scream that shrilled above the staccato drum of the huge engines.

# CHAPTER 42

I woke to the smell of bacon. Cheri and I had moved into a large bedroom at the end of the hall. I had slept the sleep of the dead, no dreams, no waking, just unconscious bliss. I got up and took a quick shower, then dressed and followed my nose to the kitchen.

Cheri was snuggled into a small lounge chair, reading the paper and drinking a cup of coffee. "Assassinated Elmer Hyden last night," she said.

Elmer Hyden was a long-time St. Croix thug and, to my memory, had been shot on three separate occasions.

"I thought he was bulletproof," Ray said, walking out of the kitchen with a glass of orange juice.

"Not anymore," Cheri said, putting down the paper and going into the kitchen to turn the bacon.

"Morning, guys," Tim said, stepping out of the west wing of the mansion.

"Where's John?" I asked.

"He was up at six, setting up his surveillance equipment," Ray said.

Like he had heard his name, John came through the front door. "Hey, Tim, can you check and see if your computer picks up my monitors."

Tim walked to the nearest computer and, with a few flicks of the keys, brought the first surveillance camera into view. "I'm getting video," he said.

"It's working," the big man said.

Tim hit a few more keys on his keyboard, and soon, eight separate surveillance pictures were on the screen

"I've got all eight video cameras," Tim said.

"Breakfast is ready," Cheri said, and we all moved toward the kitchen.

As we sat around the table, the talk turned to the case.

"We have a serious leak," Cheri said, "and I think we may be able to use it to our advantage."

"I'm listening," Ray said, leaning back.

"Somehow the killer knew we had a lab set up, and Tim was working on the case, and that spooked the killer enough to go to the college and destroy the lab." She said. "Also, I think the killer wanted to get there when Tim was gone."

We nodded.

"Would a pro that is cold as this killer have waited for Tim to leave if he thought what Tim was doing could identify him?" I asked.

"No," Ray said. "If a pro thought that Tim was moving toward an identification, he would have struck as soon as possible."

"Maybe he did; maybe he just found out where the lab was, and Tim just got lucky," I said.

"Who had that information?" Cheri said.

"Dory, us, Al," I said before Tim interrupted me.

"Tons of people at the school, teachers, administrators, students. It could have been anyone," Tim said.

"You tell people what you were doing?" Ray asked.

"I talked to some students and professors to get ideas and borrow software," Tim admitted.

"This killer is calculating, picking victims of easy opportunity," I said.

"What about Martin? That wasn't easy. Much easier just to shoot him long distance when he came out of the office. That kill and the hit and run both feel spontaneous." Cheri said.

I thought about what Cheri had said. I wasn't sure I agreed with her logic, but I had learned a long time ago to trust her gut impressions.

"More than one killer?" I asked.

"Or a very emotional killer," John said, sitting down next to me with a cup of coffee.

"Explain," I said.

"OK," John raised a finger, "the hit and run seemed to me as a random opportunity, not very well thought out. The arson is a mixed bag, maybe a meeting gone bad, maybe planned, but arson purely as a cover-up, so it doesn't smell planned. Attempts on Ziggy planned and show waiting." We had been over this ground before, but I thought a fresh, quick discussion of the killings might be helpful.

I nodded as Cheri asked, "Martin?"

"Mixed bag," John said, "the hit shows real professional skill but again, no restraint, almost an act of impulse, and again, no mean spirit, just killing. Not personal."

"None of this shows hesitation," Ray said quietly. "This person is not fully organized but experienced."

"None of the murders show cruelty," John said.

"Sam True," Cheri said.

"Wait to catch him in the pool shows surveillance or knowledge of habits. Pouring the gas in the pool and waiting for it to get to True." John said.

"Flicking in the match," I said.

"And watching him burn," I said.

Tim broke his silence and, in a calm voice, said, "I rate that as way cruel."

"Ditto," Ray said.

"So why True and not the rest of them."

"Don't forget Sue Fox was burnt," I said.

"Dead and burnt to cover up the cause," John said.

"No real pattern," I said.

"I'm liking emotional or crazy," Ray said.

"But the clear common element is StreGo." Cheri said, "And let's face it, the money is by far a compelling motive."

I finished my coffee and started collecting plates and juice glasses.

"We have to go meet Dory and then get Ziggy back here in one piece, "I said.

"You guys need me to pick up Ziggy," Ray asked.

I thought about the fact that we would have to protect Ziggy from the hospital to the safe house and asked, "You got something more important?"

Ray sat back and considered my question, "No, you're right. We need to get Ziggy here safe, and then I can do what I need to do."

"What are you thinking, Ray," John asked, bringing his dish over to the dishwasher and setting it in.

"I went over the list again last night, and I want to talk to," Ray pulled a slip of paper out of his pocket, reviewed it, and then said," Tom Severs and Allen Bower and Ann Righter."

Ray was right. We had allowed our investigation to get a little off track. Martin had given us three strong suspects, and although we had interviewed seven of the investors, we still hadn't spoken to Martin's top picks.

"Damn, we need to get out and just start beating the streets. Ray, this whole thing has got us chasing our tail." I said.

"This morning, we get Ziggy safe," Cheri said.

"This afternoon we interview the three people we haven't interviewed with the strongest motives." I said."

"Now that's a plan," Ray said.

"Tim will help me research these folks. I'll call around and get background on the three you want to interview and set up meetings while you're retrieving Ziggy," John said, and Tim nodded.

# CHAPTER 43

By noon, Ziggy was hidden at our safe house, and I was headed into town to talk to Tom Severs. Both Ann Righter and Allen Bower had left the island, but Tom Severs was working his shift with the VIPD and had agreed to meet me at the pizza café in Plaza Extra at 1:00.

I got to the little pizza bar just inside the supermarket and ordered a slice of pizza and a Coke. I was halfway through the pizza when a large, muscular black man pulled a chair out and sat down next to me.

"Mr. Cotton," he said in a gentle voice, "I've been looking forward to getting a chance to talk to you."

Tom Severs was an easy six feet two inches tall and had the build of a swimmer. He had a clean-shaven, childlike face, surprisingly bright blue eyes, and skin the color of dark-stained mahogany. As he shook my hand, his grip was strong but not forceful. Although his fellow partners had been dying off all around him, the man seemed calm and congenial.

"You know why I wanted to meet with you,' I said, setting down the remains of my pizza.

"StreGo," he said without any hesitation.

"And," I said.

"The murders of the StreGo partners."

"Yeah," I said, "the murders."

Many of the partners I had spoken to had not understood their contract with StreGo. I wanted to see Tom Sever's reaction to how the murders were impacting him, "I spoke to Attorney Shields before he was killed, and he said you own twenty-two percent of StreGo.

"Mr. Cotton," The young man said and looked into my eyes, "The company by-laws are crazy, but as a StreGo investor, I'm going to take advantage of the tragedy. I didn't make the by-laws, and when I saw how they were designed, I wished I hadn't invested, but now." He paused, gathering his thoughts, "I grew up comfortable, not like many other black kids in St. Croix. I got to go to Country Day, I got a good education, and I had good food on the table every day, but when I get that StreGo check every month, that guarantees that my kids will have something better, and I can be the servant to this community, I want to be. I don't have to take bribes as a cop to feed my family. My four boys are in private schools, not the hellholes that are the island's public schools. I think what you want to know is, am I the killer or somehow part of the killings? Isn't that true?"

"Yes," I said, watching Sever for any indication of deceit.

"The answer is no. I'm wearing this vest," he tapped his bulletproof vest, and I heard the hard metal of steel inserts in the vest. " Every day, all day. Not just when I work, but when I go to my kid's baseball game or the grocery store with my wife."

I nodded.

"I want you to catch this bastard so I can get back to my life." He said.

As I watched his movements, his eyes and heard the timber in his voice, my gut said without doubt, "This is not the killer."

"Where were you two nights ago when Mike Ziggler was shot?" I asked.

"I was on patrol with my partner on the west end," he said. My partner and I were patrolling by the fish market when the call came in.

"Who is your partner?" I asked.

"Melisa Montoya," he said, "She's out in our patrol car if you want to get verification."

"I'll walk out with you when we're done," I said.

Severs nodded.

"Do you own a small caliber pistol?" I asked.

"No, I'm not a gun guy. I own my service weapon and a twelve-gauge riot gun, and that's it."

I looked at the young man and had only one more question, "Why are you still here?"

"This is my island; I grew up here; these are my people. I'm not letting some asshole chase me away. They want to come after me, let it be."

There was no bravado in the man's words. He was stating a fact. "Your family?"

"They're up in the States with my wife's parents," he said, as he showed the first crack in his calm demeanor.

"Hard?" I said.

"Yeah, my wife and I haven't been apart a single day in our fifteen years of marriage. Yeah, it's wearing on me. Do me a favor and catch the bastard."

"I have a rule: I don't make promises," I said, "but between all the people working this case, I think the killer's going down."

Severs smiled.

# CHAPTER 44

While I was interviewing Tom Severs, Ray and Cheri called Ann Righter and Allen Bower by phone in the last few days, they both left the island, but they left contact information with Dory.

I called Cheri to get an update.

No pleasantries with Cheri, just business. "What did Severs say?" she asked when she answered my call."

"I love you too," I said.

"Yeah, Cotton, I know," she said in a flat voice that made me smile. 'What did Severs say?"

"No help, but not our guy; his partner backed his story; he was on patrol on the west end at the time of Ziggy's shooting." I pause for a second, "he's not our guy."

"Well, we're checking off candidates right and left. Ray and I made about twenty phone calls and the investors have been running from the island like green parrots during migration. Almost all the investors left the island last week before the True murder," she said.

"What are you up to?" I asked.

"Ray and I are heading east to talk to …," she paused. In the background, I could hear Ray, and then I heard Cheri's voice. After a few seconds, she was back on the phone. You need to get to the Beeston Hill Gym. Ray and I are on the way."

"What?" I asked, but I knew the answer.

"I'm not sure, Dory just said get over there," Cheri said.

I put down the phone and turned out of the grocery store's parking lot. The gym was only five minutes away.

When I got to the gym, the parking lot was full of emergency vehicles, so I parked on the side of the road. Dory was walking toward me before I even got out of my truck. I met him at the center of the road, and he led me over behind the forensic van, where we had a little privacy.

"What's up?" I asked.

"Big shit, Mad Dog, real big shit." He said, "I got a call this morning. Sonny Rone was killed in his motel room in Virgin Gorda last night, and sometime this morning, Abe Carter and Tony Morgan were killed during their morning workout."

I looked at Dory, trying to fully grasp the timeline. "Three in twenty-four hours?"

"No," Dory said, "maybe eight hours. They found Rone's body at ten o'clock, and the coroner has not gotten over from Tortola, but Rone was up, drinking at a local bar till two in the morning, so his killing had to have been after two."

"And these two," I said, pointing up at the gym.

"Between six and seven," he said, "it appears the killer shot out the surveillance cameras as he entered.

"That's pretty tight for this to be one killer," I said.

"Preliminary information from the police on Virgin Gorda is that Rone was shot once in the head with a small caliber weapon."

"Like Martin and his secretary," I said.

"Yeah."

"And Carter and Morgan?"

"Each shot once in the head with a small caliber bullet. And then the bodies were dragged into a supply closet," Dory said.

The bodies weren't discovered till around ten, but people started showing up at the gym at about seven this morning.

I shook my head; the timeline was right.

"So, the Virgin Gorda kill, and these kills are only maybe four hours apart?" I said.

"Yeah,"

"How?" I asked

"That is one mystery we do have figured out. A cigarette boat was stolen last night from Salt River Marina and found run up on the beach at Boiler's Bay. I think our killer stole the boat, ran to Virgin Gorda, killed Rone, and then ran back and killed Carter and Morgan."

"That's insane,"

"Yeah," Dory said, "insane is a good description, but the discipline to shoot three victims in the head with three shots is very professional."

Dory offered to get me into the crime scene but I saw no reason. Instead, I asked him when Cooper, the ballistics technician, would have ballistic comparisons. Dory said it would be a few days, but the ballistics were just a formality; we both knew the gun that had killed Martin Shields and Andria Chambers had killed Rone, Carter, and Morgan. The bodies were piling up, and I knew that we were not any closer to catching the killer.

"Some good news," Dory said.

I couldn't think of any good news, so I asked, "What."

"I got a call from Howard at the FBI, and they are sending a behavioral science team down. They have designated the killings as serial in nature."

In Denver and on cases in St. Croix, I had worked with the FBI and my feelings were mixed. "We're going to keep working our side," I said.

Dory nodded. "They won't let you," he said. They show up, and our little deal is out the window, you know that."

"You want the tapes back?" I asked.

"What tapes," Dory said with a sly smile.

The medical examiner was moving the bodies to the morgue van when Cheri and Ray finally walked into the parking lot and found me sitting at a bench watching the controlled chaos of the crime scene.

Cheri walked up to me and sat, and Ray hovered over me, his mass blocking the sun. "I heard the FBI is taking over the investigation," Ray said.

"Yeah," I said.

"They ain't going to be as friendly to us as Dory," he said.

"Nope," I said.

I watched three black Ford Explorers pull into the parking lot where the morgue truck had been parked only minutes ago. The first man out of the SUVs was a small compact man in the standard FBI black suit. As the compact man walked directly toward me, I had to smile. "Mike, welcome back to the island," I said.

Mike Farmer looked behind himself and, without any greeting, said, "We need to talk now."

I shrugged and pointed at the seat next to Cheri.

Mike Farmer and the three of us had a history. Before he had been transferred back to Washington, he had been the head of the FBI in the Virgin Islands. "Look," he said, "I'm going. " He stopped speaking when two other agents began to approach and turned to them.

"I told you two to wait," he snapped.

The two black-suited agents stopped in their tracks about fifteen feet away.

Agent Farmer turned his gaze back to the three of us." I don't have time to fuck around," he loudly said, "you three need to give my people everything you have and keep your noses out of this investigation. I already know that Dory is feeding you info. Understand you are not part of this investigation and if any of my superiors get any inkling that you are, I will arrest you for obstruction." He winked at us, and I winked back. Then in a much lower voice, he said. "Your numbers still the same?"

I nodded.

He took three cards out of his pocket. Each card was blank except for a phone number. "This is my number. Call it any time, day or night," he paused, looked each one of us in the eye, and gave a tight smile. Then, in a loud voice, he said, "Don't you come near my case? You three understand?"

"Yes, sir, "Ray said a little too loudly.

Cheri and I just nodded, and Agent Farmer walked quickly back toward the gym door, letting the two other agents catch up with him.

"Quit smiling, you idiot," Cheri said to Ray, who had an ear-to-ear grin on his face, and the grin turned into a fake frown.

"Nothing we can do here," I said.

"Nope," Ray said, "The FBI is on the job."

# CHAPTER 45

From the vacant shed the killer watched it all. The emergency vehicles pouring into the parking lot, Mad Dog Cotton meeting with Detective Dory Hancock, the arrival of Cheri Cotton and Ray Jones and finally the arrival of the FBI. The killer knew what would happen next, the FBI would flood the island with agents. Marks would be put into protection. Individuals like the Cotton's and Detective Hancock would be forced to sit on the sidelines.

 The FBI would turn the investigation into a zoo, and the killer would miss the challenge the three private investigators offered. They had been wild cards, unpredictable in their tactics, and fun to match wits with. On the other hand, the FBI, as it had proven to the killer many times before, would be predictable and easy to manipulate.

The killer thought about the videos that had been destroyed at the college. The plan was moving along perfectly.  By now, the FBI would be arranging to get copies of the videos and discovering the secrets the videos held. The killer snickered at that thought. Tomorrow, they would be looking for the wrong person, a dead man.

# CHAPTER 46

By the time we got back to the safe house, the sun was setting in the west, and the front porch of the mansion offered a perfect view.

"Damn," I said looking over the expansive view and the brilliant yellows and oranges that painted the western sky, "I love this place."

"You just like the cheap beer," Cheri said as she handed me a cold Heineken out of the cooler beside her.

"And the scantily clad nubile young females," I added.

"Yeah," she said, "like you could keep up,"

"I keep up with you," I said.

"Touché," Ray said taking a long pull off his beer.

"You trust Farmer? "I asked.

"I never liked that guy before, but after last year, yeah, I trust him; he's in a bad spot. The FBI won't like him keeping us in the loop and working with us, but I admire he's working with us."

Cheri squirmed down in her lounger and, in a faraway voice, said, "Being a federal agent is hard; the rules you have to follow are there for a reason, but when bodies are stacking up, you just want results. You guys know that if Farmer's bosses get wind that he's working with Dory and us behind their backs, they'll send him to Alaska to count polar bears."

"Naw," Ray said, "they will make him Director, it's the government, the bigger the fuck up, the further you advance."

I didn't understand why, but we all laughed.

"Hey guys, a voice came from the sliding door. I got the downloads ready to go to Agent Farmer. Do you want me to send my work with the video or not?"

"Just the video," I said. Their people will find their own way to work with it."

"How about my reformatted stuff." He asked.

"Yeah," Cheri yelled, "send the stuff you reformatted. That will maybe speed things along for them."

The glass door slid shut, and Ray said, "The FBI sees how smart that young man is; they are likely to steal him from us."

We all sat silent looking as the brilliance of the sunset just kept filling the sky.

"It ever dawn on you guys, this killer is playing us for fools," Ray said.

"How so?" I asked.

"All the weirdness: the organized and then unorganized style of the kills: the missing of easy shots with a long gun and pin-point accuracy of the small caliber gun. The different methods of the kills. Some kills cruel, some planned, some unplanned."

"What's your point?" I asked.

"What if the key to the killer's personality is this is all planned out, all set up to drive the behavioral guys nuts, what if all the inconsistency is the consistency? Designed to throw us off track."

"It's a little too Steven King for me," I said. I've worked with dozens of killers over the years, and they don't plan like that; they are more direct."

"If our killer is military or a cop, they will know what to show us and how to confuse us," I said.

"And," Ray added, "no one is more predictable than the FBI."

"You're saying the FBI intervention is what the killer expected,"

"But we have an advantage, a wild card," Cheri said.

Ray and I looked at her. That sneaky look was on her face.

"There is no way that the killer could guess that Agent Farmer would still be working with us under the table." She said.

"If he's been playing us, he will know to expect the classic FBI takeover of the case."

"So, we can't let the killer know we're still on the case," Ray said.

"We need to do things that we would do if we were off the case," I said with a smile.

"Ziggy needs to fire us." Ray said," And go into FBI protection."

"Can they protect him?" I asked.

"As well as us," Cheri said.

"OK," I said, "we need to be seen around and can't do any investigation that leads the killer to think we are still working the case."

"No more interviews," I said.

"No more open contact with Dory," Cheri said.

"What about Antonio Mendoza," Ray said.

"We keep that contact; he won't deal with the FBI," Ray said.

"I agree," I said, "everything else has to be on the sly. We have no idea who the killer or killers are, so we have to act like we're off the case.

"Do we go back to the boat?" Cheri asked.

"Life as usual," Ray said.

"What about the kid," I asked, "and John?"

"I don't think the killer knows about this place. I say we leave them here, and Tim can continue to work on getting an ID. I think he is damn sharp and off the wall enough that he may come up with something."

"Leave John for protection just in case," Ray said.

Cheri nodded

"Well, let's go tell the boss it's time to fire us," I said.

"Damn," Ray said, "fired again."

# CHAPTER 47

My idea was simple: Let the killer think that we were off the case and that the FBI was the only investigation being conducted.

We agreed that somehow, the killer was getting intelligence on our activities and actions, like the burning of evidence at the school, and might continue to follow us if we were openly investigating the case. By going underground, it was my hope we could add a level of investigation to Mike Farmer's pursuit of the killer. Mike understood St. Croix and understood that many standard police procedures would not work in the tight-knit community, where secrets were very hard to keep.

We kept Tim and John under wraps at the safe house. Cheri and I announced to everyone that we were taking the boat to St. Thomas and cruising out of Green Key Marina. Ray announced that he was leaving the island for a while and climbed on a plane to San Juan. Mike Farmer made a formal statement that the FBI had taken Ziggy into protective custody.

The day after the FBI announced it was taking over the case, all of us arrived back on St. Croix by private yacht and were back at the safe house. Ray had found us three new, clean vehicles with blacked-out windows.

When Cheri and I arrived at the safe house we were exhausted. We had met Silvia Moore, the owner of a small cruising yacht five miles offshore. Her captain had taken our boat, Itchy Feet, to Puerto Rico, where I had arranged to have the boat hauled and worked on in a small yard on the east end of the island. Silvia then brought us back to Green Key Marina and docked her boat. At four in the morning, Ray had picked up Cheri and me from the marina in one of our "new" cars.

When we walked in, John was monitoring the surveillance cameras and gave us a finger to the lips signal to be quiet. He pointed to the couch, where a pajama-clad Tim lay snoring quietly.

We nodded and quietly went to our separate rooms.

About eight in the morning, I woke and came out into the great room which Cheri had begun calling the war room. Tim was still sleeping on the couch, and Ray and John were sipping coffee in the kitchen.

"Morning," I whispered and poured myself a cup of coffee. As I sipped, I looked over at our sleeping computer expert.

"Was up from the time you guys' left till about an hour before you got back, but he's got some stuff that may make a difference," John said in a whisper.

I nodded.

"What's the game plan?" Ray asked.

"First, let's see if Tim has any more leads," I said. " Hiding out is critical," I explained. The feds will freeze us out if they find out Mike is using us to do his dirty work, and if the killer knows we're still on the case, he may start hunting us down."

"Fine with me," Ray said, "he tries to hunt me down, and this thing will be over quick."

"Yeah, man," John said, giving Ray a loud high-five.

From the couch, Tim sat up startled, "What, what the fu…." He looked at Ray and John and began to wipe the sleep out of his eyes. "Jesus, guys, you scared the crap out a me."

Ray and John grinned at him unapologetically.

"Coffee time, my man," Ray said, raising the half-empty pot.

Tim made a wide gesture with his hands and said, "Big cup, Mr. Ray. I need the juice."

"Back to the plan," John said as Tim stumbled to the counter to get his coffee.

"The way I see it, we let the FBI and maybe VIPD take over the leg work, interviews, shit like that. The reality is they are good at that kind of stuff and at doing what you've been doing, Tim. They have guys who scan through videos for a living, so let them."

"And us?" Ray asked.

"We light as many fires as we can to smoke the bastard out," I said.

"Define fires," a voice said from behind me.

I turned, and Cheri stood behind me, her hair wet from the shower. In an attempt to look less intimidating, she had on my "I EAT SHARK FOR LUNCH" tee shirt, blue jeans, and her new pink sneakers. It was a very sexy look.

"John wanted to hear what the plan is," I said.

"I got that part and the fact that we're the outlaws in this little game." She crossed her arms and repeated, "Define fires."

I looked down. I had hoped to get all the guys on board before I let my plan out of the bag, but it appeared now I had to man up and let the cat out of the bag without the guy's support.

I had paused, trying to regroup my argument and soften it for Cheri, when she repeated a third time, "Define fire."

Ray slid a cup of coffee across to her, but she kept her eyes on me.

As a rule, when I have a really hair-brained idea, I try to break it to Cheri slowly. It's hard to have the person you love tell you you're an idiot.

She fixed me with her eyes, and a wet ringlet of damp hair fell across her forehead. She sipped her coffee and looked into my eyes. "Fire?" she asked.

I swallowed and began. "The FBI can do the leg…"

"I heard that, Mad Dog," she said, "I want to hear this plan, this fire."

"We use the island thugs to find the killer's vehicle," I said.

"Are you nuts," Ray said, "They'll turn this island into a shooting gallery. Do you have any idea how many white trucks are on this rock!"

"Fuck, Mad Dog, some crazy bastard like Mendoza finds out the person trying to kill him is driving a white truck. He will not be safe." John said.

I had laid awake all night working on my plan, and in the face of Ray and John's response, I was about to say, "OK, bad idea." When…

Cheri spoke in a quiet voice. "I like it. I like it a lot."

We all looked at her, dumbfounded, except Tim, who raised his hand like a schoolboy.

Cheri turned her gaze from me to Tim, and we all moved our attention with her. Tim sat, the steaming cup of coffee perched in one hand and the other hand raised. When we turned, he smiled and said. "Not just the truck. I may have a fairly accurate sketch of the killer."

When none of us said anything, he continued, "It's not a great sketch, but I was able to take points from the truck windows and make a rough compilation of the killer face."

"Show me," Cheri said, moving toward the computers.

Tim sat down at one of the computers, and we sat behind him. "The tint on the truck's glass is heavy, so you only get glimpses of who is in the truck when the light is perfect. Last night, I went through all the videos that identified the truck and pulled out the best 200 video freeze screens."

A screen appeared with thumbnail photos of the cab of the white truck. "I then studied each photo to see if the lighting allowed us to see something of the driver." The screen changed and only eight photos remained. "These eight had images from the truck that were identifiable."

Tim blew up one of the photos. "This is the best photo I had of the driver."

"I don't see shit," Ray said.

"Look closely," Tim said, and like four seagulls eyeing a thrown piece of trash, we all leaned forward. Tim put his pencil on the screen and traced a very vague shape.

"Doesn't do much for me, man," Ray said.

The screen changed, and another photo of the black truck window appeared. "Same," John said as he reached forward with his finger, going to the screen.

"No," Tim said, and John pulled his finger back, "not the same."

Tim again traced the hidden figure. "I know they both look the same," he said, "but when I break down the actual photo pixels and subject the two photos to different degrees of light and color in my video editing program, the two photos can be manipulated to this."

The screen went from black and white to green and purple. The purple was a line, the outline of a face. You couldn't tell who it was, but you could tell it was a face.

Ray pushed in and stared, "That's a face?" he said.

"Yep," Tim said. He began manipulating the keys and speaking as a series of cleared pictures came up on the screen. "I spent most of last night putting the ten good photos I mentioned earlier and came up with this."

Tim hit a final key, and a blurred face appeared.

"That may be good enough that someone can recognize the killer," I said.

The figure, although blurred, showed a black man with a short-cropped beard and mustache wearing a baseball cap. The side view Tim had managed to pull from the tinted windows was clearer. It showed the man to have rounded, high cheekbones and a large, distinctly crooked nose. The view from the front showed close-set eyes, a full mouth, and a narrow forehead. The nose again was distinctly shaped, wide toward the bottom and narrow toward the top. From the front, the baseball cap displayed the classic NY symbol of the New York Yankees.

I looked at the photo for a long minute, the killer's face seemed odd, but I couldn't put my finger on it. "How accurate is this, Tim?" I asked.

"You need to think of it as a composite sketch," Tim explained. "The computer picks up pixel color and light variances from the reflection in the tinted window and uses those variances to add to a composite map of the face. The photo will get better as I am able to add more clues to the composite from more photos."

"What can we trust as accurate in this composite?" Cheri asked.

Tim thought for a second, "Gender, race, facial hair, and the Yankee ball cap are clear. I think the side view is much more accurate than the front view. The nose is composed of pixels from five photos; it should be fairly accurate. Using this system, the outline of the face is far more accurate.

"It's a start," I said.

"Tim," Cheri said, "Would you be comfortable sharing this with the FBI? Possibly, their people can get a more accurate composite."

"No problem. I'm sure they have much better resources than I have. I'm kind of flying by the seat of my pants here." Tim said with a slight shrug of his shoulders.

"OK, we send all of Tim's composite work to Mike and we take the truck to the street."

"Antonio Mendoza," Ray said.

"And someone who can give this to the boys at Kennedy. They have a stake in this. Sam True was one of them. They will want revenge," I said.

"I can arrange that, but how do we keep the thugs from killing every poor bastard on the island with a white truck?" John asked.

"Make it clear that the dents I found on the truck have to match perfectly," Tim said.

"Offer a bounty for the identification of the truck, but make it clear that the thugs who find it don't get a cent unless they call us and we identify the truck," John said.

"We can pull the reward out of our slush fund. Ziggy put money in it today." Cheri said.

"Ten thousand will be enough to get them to call us," Ray said.

"Tim, you still got things to do?" I asked.

"Tons of stuff, I'm still finding and reformatting new video," he said.

"John," I said, turning to the big man, "would you mind staying and keeping watch over the safehouse?"

"Done," he said.

"I want to stay here. I need to build a matrix of all the tier two and three owners and get photos of them." Cheri said.

I looked at Ray and said, "I guess that leaves you and me to set fires."

"Yeah," Ray said, "my specialty."

# CHAPTER 48

Things had changed in Antonio Mendoza's compound. As we pulled onto the dirt road leading to it, I spotted two men semi-hidden in the bush. Each man carried an assault rifle.

"Mr. Mendoza has become security conscious," Ray said, keeping his eyes fixed on the road.

I looked briefly at the young man partially hidden by the thick bush. "Yep," I said, waving at the skinny little kid with the big assault rifle.

Seeing my wave, the boy crouched down and moved back into the bush.

"Something's wrong," Ray said, "That little shit back there can't be thirteen."

"New recruits," I said as we rounded the corner and came into the dirt lot in front of Mendoza's main house.

Three hard-looking men stepped out of the cover of the outbuildings and leveled assault rifles at Ray's SUV.

"Not good," Ray said calmly, laying his big 44 pistol in his lap.

The three men began to advance, and I watched as the man nearest to me thumbed the safety off his weapon. I smiled my "It's OK" smile and raised my hands.

The gunman gave me the "Roll down your window" hand gesture.

Because the window was offering me little or no protection, I rolled down my window.

"Get out," the man ordered. I heard Ray's door open as I opened mine.

When I stepped out, the man spun me and expertly lifted my Glock from my waistband. From the other side of the truck I heard Ray say, "If I give you this, you promise to take care of it?"

"Don't be an asshole," one of the guards said from Ray's side of the truck, "just give me the cannon and assume the position."

It occurred to me that these three were not your normal thugs.

"How ya been, Kiki," Ray said.

"Fine, Ray, you got anything else on ya?" the gunman asked.

"Just this, oh yeah, and this," Ray said.

I looked over, and Ray was handing the third gunman two small pistols.

"Search them both," the man Ray had called Kiki said.

The gunman on my side kicked my legs apart, pressed me to the SUV's hood, and ran his hands over my body, easily finding the twenty-five-caliber pistol in my right front pocket and the switchblade taped to my arm.

"Shame on you," the gunman said as he ripped the knife, duct tape, and all from my wrist.

"Ouch," I said, "be gentle. It took years to grow that hair."

From the door, the woman who had been with Mendoza earlier in the week yelled at the three men, "They clean?"

"They are now," the man named Kiki yelled back.

"Bring them in," she yelled.

The gunman on my side pushed me, and I turned to look at him. He was a hard-looking Hispanic man with a small scar under his right eye and a stab mark under his chin. His eyes were cold and had lizard intelligence that spelled pure dangerous. Everything about him screamed professional. I tried to envision him as the killer shooting Martin and his secretary. "Yeah," I thought, looking into his eyes, "this guy could do it."

"I got an envelope in the truck I need to give Mr. Mendoza," I said.

The gunman pushed me forward and pulled the envelope out of the truck. "This?" he said, holding it up.

"Yeah,"

Without taking the barrel of the assault rifle from the center of my chest, he ran his left hand over the envelope, checking for a weapon. Satisfied, he handed the envelope to me and smiled, "Now let's go," he said, pushing me forward.

"Ray walked over to me when I rounded the front of the SUV and said, "Mad Dog, meet Kiki Rivera."

I eyed the tall, athletic Hispanic man following Ray. "Mr. Mad Dog," he said with a nod of his head.

# CHAPTER 49

Antonio Mendoza lay in a nest of blankets propped up by pillows. His right arm was in a sling. Sitting next to him was Sal McFiester, a local veterinarian. The swarthy Puerto Rican was pale, and the lump of dreadlocks around his brow was soaked in sweat.

"Looking a little peaked, brother," Ray said when the three guards brought us in front of Mendoza.

''Been a rough week," he said with a weak smile.

"Shot?" I asked.

Mendoza waited a second and then said, " Are you bringing me a present?" He stared at the manila envelope that I was holding.

"Our computer guy pulled these off some videos. We think it's the killer's truck." I said.

Mendoza held up his good arm, and the guard next to me took the envelope from me and handed it to Mendoza.

Mendoza handed the envelope to his girlfriend. She pulled the six photos Tim had made from the envelope and handed the photos to Mendoza. He sat up and started putting the photos on the coffee table in front of him.

"The truck is dinged up pretty good," I said.

"I see that," Mendoza said, concentrating on the truck photos. "I'll get these out to the street."

"We were hoping there wouldn't be a white truck blood bath out there," Ray said.

Mendoza spoke quietly and firmly, "My people know this prick is mine." He looked up at me and said, "I'll make sure it's our guy. " He paused and smiled without finishing his statement.

"Bring him in alive, and there's a ten K reward," Ray said.

"I make that much in a good day. I think I'll pass on the reward," Mendoza said calmly as he laid back down.

"When we have something else, we'll bring it to you," I said.

Mendoza gave me a long look and then said, "Thank you. In return, I will put these photos out on the street. Hopefully, someone can help us find this madman."

I turned to leave, and Mendoza spoke, "Mr. Cotton," I turned back, and the small, thin man was staring at me, "I appreciate what you and Mr. Jones are doing."

I nodded.

Kiki and his two buddies led us back to the car and gave us our guns back with a sack of ammunition they had taken out of the guns.

As we drove away from the compound, Ray kept looking forward as he spoke, "I have always thought Mendoza was tied to the Puerto Rico gangs. Now I know he is. Kiki is an enforcer for one of the big Puerto Rican bosses. He and his men must be on loan to Mendoza."

"How do you know him," I asked.

Ray just smiled and drove to the parking lot of a gas station, where we separated out the ammunition in the sack and loaded our guns.

"What now?" Ray asked, his black sunglasses staring forward.

"We wait."

## CHAPTER 50

We didn't have to wait long. Ray and I had only driven about ten miles when my cell phone rang. It was Mike Farmer.

"Did you read the paper today," he asked

"Nope," I said.

"Get one, an Avis," he said, "third page, read it and call me back."

I pointed over to the Plaza Extra we were driving by and told Ray to pull in.

"What's up?" he asked as I climbed out of the SUV and ran into the store.

I bought the last two Avis newspapers in the stand and hurried back to where Ray was double-parked.

"What's up?" he repeated.

I thumbed to the third page of the local paper and began looking. On the bottom right corner I found what I was looking for. The ad was in bold letters. It said:

### STAY WITH

### StreGo AND DIE WITH StreGo

### SELL OR DIE

I showed Ray the ad.

Ray looked at it for a long time before he spoke. "Fuckin weird."

I called Mike Farmer.

"Hello, Mike," I said, "I don't know what to tell you except it's damn weird."

"My agents just got back from the Avis office and the ad was sent to the Avis with payment yesterday. No one knows shit about who sent it."

"Did you get the envelope and the original ad?" I asked.

"Yeah, we overnighted it to our lab in Florida." Mike said, "It's on the fast track, but we won't have anything until tomorrow or maybe the next day."

"Get ahold of an officer at VIPD and ask him how the owners communicate if they want to sell. The Corporate By-Laws are set up so you can only sell to an existing owner in your tier."

"Have you seen the By-Laws?" Mike asked.

"No, but the lawyer explained them to me before he was killed. I'm telling you that there must be a way for the owners to find buyers in their tier." I said.

"No one told me this," he said, anger growing in his voice.

"Dory didn't fill you in?" I asked.

"No, fuck no. We need to talk, Cotton. We need to talk right now."

I looked at Ray, who I knew could hear pieces of the conversation, and he gave me a big smile.

"Meet me where we met before," I said, winking at Ray.

"How long?"

"I can be there in ten minutes," I said.

"I'm maybe fifteen," he said.

"Why don't they just ask Ziggy?" Ray said when I hung up.

"They probably moved him off the island," I said.

"If you were them, wouldn't you have debriefed him before you let him leave the island?"

I thought about what Ray said, and it made sense.

# CHAPTER 51

Nearly two years earlier, in the middle of the kidnapping case that had involved Ray's goddaughter, we had met Agent Mike Farmer at the large pavilion by the Old Christiansted Fort. We had chosen the location because it was an open area, and everyone would be safer. Today, the tables were switched, and the openness of the area seemed exposed as Ray and I stood waiting for the FBI agent to show. The killer liked shooting long distances from cover, and the many vacant buildings around the open park offered way too many good sniper positions.

Ray was in constant motion. The black mirrors of his sunglasses were scanning the hundreds of places where a sniper could be hiding.

"Relax, Ray, first, how would the killer know to be here and second, we'll be out of here before anyone could set up," I said.

"You believe that," Ray said, "I believe this guy has an inside track and is good enough to set up in a matter of minutes."

Mike Farmer arrived and parked in the Old Fort's parking lot. He climbed out of his black SUV and walked briskly across the green expanse of the park to the pavilion. "Bad idea, guys," he said when he was within speaking distance. "Let's ride, we can take my SUV."

We all walked back to the SUV and climbed in. I got in the back and let Ray sit in front. I began to relax as the big, black government vehicle pulled into traffic and turned toward the island's east end.

"OK," Farmer said, "help me, what's going on?"

"You haven't debriefed Ziggy?" Ray asked.

"No," Farmer said, "We fucked up. I was in a hurry to get him into protection, and we got him off the island an hour after you turned him over."

Ray shook his head, and from the back seat, I could sense his growing frustration. "You don't understand the StreGo…."

I interrupted Ray, "Mike, what Ray's getting at is that if you don't understand the nuances of the StreGo corporate structure, you can't understand this case."

"I got it, I'm fucking up," Mike said, "now that said, let me know what I need to know."

I wondered where to start and decided to start from the beginning.

Two hours later, we had made three loops around the east end of the island and one loop out to Hovensa. During this time, I talked, and Ray added important parts of the investigation.

Mike had explained that the FBI had been informed of the killings of Martin Shields, his secretary, and the last three victims, who were all killed by the small caliber handgun. That was the "serial killings" that had caused the FBI to take jurisdiction, and the file he and his people had been sent by the upper management of the Virgin Islands government only had those cases attached. I remembered Dory's frustration with the Chief and the Commissioner when they had refused to declare the case a serial killing and tie the cases together when the first killings took place. Now they had covered their own incompetent asses by not putting all the murders tied to StreGo together. Instead, they had used the five handgun shootings MO to form the base of their request for FBI help in the case.

"Didn't you get a clue things were fucked up when you got a bunch of oddball videos," Ray asked, unable to hide his anger.

"We just turned them over to techs and said, do your thing," Mike said.

"Well, welcome back to the island," I said. You've been back for less than a day and have already been bit by the St. Croix cover-my-ass bug."

Mike shook his head, "After five years working here and having those idiots fuck up cases, I should have expected something like this," he said.

"Damn straight, you should have. All that easy time in Washington made you soft," Ray said.

I laid my hand on Ray's shoulder to calm him down and said, "That's the case as we see it. Mike, Cheri, and I have a full set of work notes on the interviews, and Cheri is working on a matrix of StreGo suspects we interviewed and their alibis. We have been able to develop good, strong alibis for about fifteen of the second—and third-tier suspects, but if there are two killers or maybe a bad alibi, any of the fifteen could still be the killer."

"I do have one more little thing I need to share," I said.

I told Mike about Antonio Mendoza and our intention to inform the criminal organization at the Kennedy Project about the truck.

When I finished, Mike was quiet for a long time and then said, "That should shake the tree,"

For the first time in the hours we had been driving around, Ray's sour mood lightened. "Them bad boys won't just shake the tree. They will probably cut it down."

For the second time that day, I found myself laughing about something that wasn't the least bit funny.

# CHAPTER 52

The killer smiled; the bug in the FBI agent's car was working perfectly. She felt a certain excitement in knowing the group of detectives Ziggler had hired were still on the case. It had been a smart move for them to act like they were off the case, but good intelligence always trumped smart moves. She still didn't know where the safe house was and wondered if she should have recorded the conversation between the Agent and the detectives and taken the time to bug Ray Jones' SUV parked at the Old Fort.

"You can't do everything," she thought.

Her mind turned to the newspaper ad, she loved it, what a great red herring. She wondered who had published the ad. Whoever it was, they had signed their death warrant. She knew the FBI had a good chance of identifying the idiot, and when they did, she would kill the son of a bitch quickly while they did their bureaucratic square dance. The great thing about the FBI was they did so much ass-covering that they moved very slow, and she moved fast. The detectives were different. They had no bureaucratic hurdles. She had to hustle to stay ahead of them.

She had not listened to the bug on Detective Dory Hancock's phone since the FBI had taken over the case. She hit a few keys on the computer, and a GPS tracker of his car showed his movements. There was nothing important there.

The truck and the crazy detective using the thugs to track the truck had been a surprise. She would have to leave the truck in the locked garage. It had been her husband's and the irony of using his truck had made her feel powerful, like she was doing what he would have done. She felt a tear thinking about him; it had been years since she had been forced to kill him, and the hole in her heart had never healed. She hated losing the truck, but the detectives had won that little battle.

Absently, she itched the base of her neck. The false beard had caused a rash on her neck and the makeup had caused a minor eruption of acne on her face. The skin irritation was minor, considering the ruse had sent the entire army of investigators looking for a bearded man. She felt the power of her brilliance. She was invincible. She would kill them all if it took ten years, they would all die. They were, after all, just a covey of money-hungry drug dealers, and their greed had been the tool that had snuffed out Charlie's life. "You kill my son, and I kill you," she thought. She looked at the wall above her desk where hundreds of photos and news articles were displayed; for years, she had solved dozens of crimes with her murder board. Now, she used a murder board to commit them.

She sat back and said, "OK, who to kill today." Much of her prey had fled the island, but many were still foolishly clinging to their little insignificant lives. She took her laser pointer and scanned the wall stopping on the smiling face of a young police officer. She smiled and rose from her chair.

# CHAPTER 53

The text came at three in the morning.

"Got another one," the text from Mike Farmer said, "Meet me 4."

Cheri rubbed her eyes and looked at the screen.

"Who?" she asked.

"This is all we got," I said, looking at the strange text.

"Meet me 4, what's that."

I went to my wallet and pulled out the card that the Agent had given me. The card was for Duggan's Restaurant, a seafood restaurant on the east end.

Our safe house was only five miles from Duggan's, and Cheri, Ray, and I got to the empty ocean-side building before Farmer. The bar and restaurant were open-air, and the owner left the seating area open. We walked across the small wooden bridge and down the stone path to the open front entrance. Two lights that shined on the deck that overlooked the beach dimly lit the interior of the restaurant. I could hear the waves lapping under the north side of the building and the large deck. The sliding glass door to the north side of the building was open, and the three of us walked out onto the lit deck.

"You call him?" Ray asked, looking out onto the moonlit ocean.

"No answer," I said.

I heard the scratch of sandy footsteps on wood, and a dark figure appeared at the side of the building. The figure, still in shadow, started climbing the steps to the deck. Mike Farmer's compact frame emerged from the shadows. He was clad in black pants and a long-sleeve black pullover. On his right hip was his Glock 40 Caliber pistol.

He walked to the rail of the deck where the three of us stood.

After a few minutes, Framer held up a small device that all three of us recognized immediately.

Ray took the device and examined it.

"Tech found it in my SUV, it's deactivated."

"GPS and Audio, this is a nice piece," Ray said, handing the stainless disc back to the agent.

"We ran the registration numbers. It was sold to DEA, and DEA says it was given to the Virgin Islands Police Department to do internal surveillance."

"Came from VIPD inventory?" Ray asked.

"They showed it still in inventory," Farmer said, a little anger sliding out.

"Our little ride around?" I asked.

Farmer shook his head.

"The killer may have," he paused and reconsidered his statement, "probably heard everything."

"My thugs looking for the truck?" Ray said.

"The fact we're still on the case," Cheri said.

I nodded.

"It gets worse," Farmer said. VIPD got ten small surveillance cameras and fifteen of these. " He held up the small black disk. They are all missing from the chief's office."

"He kept it in his office?" I asked.

"Seems so," he answered.

"Twenty-five devices. Can we scan for them?" I asked.

"My tech is waiting. He will scan your vehicles."

Ray looked around the dark beach and into the blackness of the restaurant. "The killer knows we're here," he said, moving back into the shadow of the building.

"I say we go inside," Cheri said.

She was right. The open deck seemed very exposed. We moved back into the darkness of the closed main dining room and sat at one of the tables.

"Now what?" I asked.

"My tech found three devices, two in cars and one in my office. We were working on sweeping all the federal buildings when we got the call from Dory on a homicide."

"Who?" I asked.

"Mia Trecker, a VIPD officer that liaisons with the schools was at a late-night meeting with the principal of Country Day. When she came out of the building, the killer shot her once in the head. We've taken five video feeds into custody, and I'll want that kid of yours to look at the copies we're making. He's pretty good at what he's doing. My techs were really impressed by what he sent over."

"Small caliber?" Ray asked.

"Yeah, Cooper is doing an examination right now, but yeah, it's the same weapon. The silencer leaves a distinct mark on the bullets."

"Anything else?" I asked.

"My techs are working the scene, but I'd say no."

"She was a second-tier owner, " I said, remembering the name.

Farmer nodded.

"She was a nice kid," Cheri said as I saw tears roll down her cheek. "We worked together on the Biden protection detail."

"You knew her," Ray said.

"Yeah," Cheri said angrily, wiping the tear away, "she was finishing her degree online. She wanted to apply for the Marshal Service," she paused, "damn, I hate this case."

"We need to use these devices to feed the killer false information, set the son of a bitch up," Ray said.

"Great idea, but real hard to pull off," Farmer said.

I could hear the words that the other people at the table were saying, but I didn't comprehend them. My mind was in its own world, swirling with all the facts, swirling with all the information that I knew was hiding the truth in plain sight.

"Cotton, you with us," Farmer said.

"No," I said, "I have to go. I'll be on my phone."

"Mad Dog," Cheri said,

I stood up and raised my hand to stop Cheri, "I've got to go." I said. My head was spinning. I needed time, time to myself, time to think. I walked out to the deck and down the wooden stairs to the beach. A two-foot surf was splashing against the soft sand. I began to walk.

# CHAPTER 54

As I walked, my mind buzzed. I remember walking down the beach, the moonlight, traffic, and bright lights coming at me and passing me, but mostly, I remember walking— miles and miles of walking.

I stopped and stood, confused. The bee swarm of thoughts that had crowded my head was gone. I sensed light and turned. The sun's rays had begun to filter dawn light into the eastern sky. The high eastern sky was awash with red-orange spilling across the cloud-etched sky.

I stood on a grassy hillside. I looked down at my hands. They were scratched and bloody. I remembered the fence. I remembered climbing over the fence. I saw bloody scratches on my hand. I thought, *"Odd, I saw the blood, but I couldn't feel the pain."* I looked up, and for the first time in hours, I recognized where I was.

The dawn lit the edges of the pool. I walked to the edge and looked down. The large leaves of a nearby grape tree scattered across the bottom of the pool and made a faint grating sound against the concrete as the light wind gently scooted the dried husks.

*"Empty,"* my mind tumbled the word around, trying to turn it into a thought.

Then, the scent hit me. Faint as a single spider web spun and floated free in the breeze. My gut clenched as the faint stench of burnt flesh moved into me like an oily poison.

I froze, eyes peering into the darkness of the pool, fixed on the shadows of the slithering leaves as the bottom, in the inky shadows. A cool breeze touched the hairs on my neck, and a rush of chill ran down my neck.

For a split second, my world froze. My eyes saw the straight white walls of the empty pool fading into dim, dark shadows. My ears heard the scratching from the leaves that scooted in the dim bottom of the hole. My nose fogged with the unmistakable scent of burnt flesh.

My skin felt touched with a cold, merciless chill. Was it born from a tease of wind? My heart stopped, a beat of my life skipped, and the breeze touched my neck and chilled its way down my spine.

I sensed the first putrid drops of bile as they slid under my tongue. I felt a primal fear.

I felt my tired body sway and, with a start, caught my balance. The feeling had passed, but the taste of bile was still strong, and the faint scent of burnt flesh still lingered.

I forced my mind clear and realized I was standing on the lawn of the mansion where Sam True had died.

With new eyes, I looked at the empty pool. "*Empty,*" my mind tossed the words back and forth. I looked up at the main house, the large veranda where San True's new wife had sat.

It was all empty now; that big house, the fine yard, the majestic view felt … My mind searched for a word but all that came was "*empty.*"

"*She gone,*" I thought.

What had her name been? I searched my foggy memory. She had an odd name, a name that rhymed with Sam. That was it, "Tam, Tam True."

The faint scent of death by burning hung in my mind like a thin strand, fragile but going somewhere, trying to awaken a thought.

I spoke the words before my mind grasped the idea. "She killed him," I said.

Like a movie playing before me, I saw the small, petite, brown-skinned woman kneeling at the pool, the gas, then the flame.

It made no sense, but I knew it was true.

I remembered a smell, a smell that I had never identified before. I had been on the veranda thinking, "*I should say something to her.*" I had smelled the burnt flesh, but it had been mingled with a sweet-flowered perfume—her perfume.

She had said, "I feel like the smell is inside me. I can't get the smell of burning hair out of my mind. Oh god, that smell, it's like it's in me,"

I remembered the words and that sickening sweet smell of the mix of death and perfume.

I turned and looked at the blood-red sunrise that had now flowed and erupted over the sky all across the horizon.

"There had been a strong breeze," I said, "a strong easterly."

I looked the seventy yards up the hill to the veranda. The mansion was straight south from the pool!

The pieces started to fall into place.

Her motive was money, lots of money if she didn't know about the StreGo Bi Laws.

She had opportunity. One of us had said the killer had to know Sam True's habit of going to the pool for sunrise. Who knew that better than his wife? She knew where the gas was. Finally, the clincher is that this crime was a personal and cruel act of someone who hated Sam True.

I thought about the hundreds of homicides I had worked. The wife should have always been the first suspect. The string of StreGo murders had thrown us off the scent of the real killer. Tam True had killed Sam True. I knew the truth.

I ripped my cell phone from my pocket and began to run as I speed-dialed Cheri and pushed the speaker so I could keep running.

"Where the fuck are you?" she said when the phone rang.

"I'll explain," I yelled as I reached the road and began running down the hill toward the Choy guard shack. "Get Ray, you two need to meet me at the Buccaneer."

I was walking down the Buccaneer's main drive and out of breath when our truck came into view. I stopped and waited, trying to catch my breath.

Cheri stopped in front of me and looked at me through the rolled-down window. "Are you OK?" She asked.

"Yeah," I said, getting in and trying to catch my breath.

"You look like shit,"

I looked up at her, " I know who the killers are." I blurted out.

"Killers," she said.

"Yeah," I said, "killers. Take me to the boat. I need a shower and to change clothes. It's gonna be a long day"

I called Ray and let him know I was with Cheri, and we would meet him at the boat.

# CHAPTER 55

I was clean, and even though I hadn't slept in a day, I felt invigorated.

We sat at our favorite table at the Deep End restaurant; Beth, our favorite waitress, was bringing the pot over to fill our cups. "Breakfast will be out in a few minutes," she said as she filled our cups.

When she was out of earshot, Ray said, "Tam True," he shook his head, "I will be damned if she said that you're right. There is no way she would have smelled the fire."

"Not unless she set it," Cheri said. "And I'm sure we checked Madge Thomas off the list based on her alibi for the Sam True murder."

"The person in the car is a guy," Ray said.

"No," Cheri said thoughtfully and then looked up at me, "remember her rash?"

I thought of our second meeting, the peeling rash on her skin, the way she had itched and flicked the skin away. "Fuck, glue from a fake beard."

"What," Ray said, setting his coffee down.

"When we met with Madge the second time, we came to confront her about Sam True's murder; she had an air-tight alibi," Cheri explained.

Ray nodded.

"During the interview, she kept scratching a rash on her neck and peeling off dead skin. It was kind of an ugly rash, blotchy, like the skin had been pulled away. I told her I had a salve that might help."

Ray looked at both of us and then said, "Glue for a false beard,"

"She's a cop; she knows about video surveillance, so she went in disguise," I said.

"As a man," Ray said.

"As a man," Cheri confirmed.

We stopped talking while Beth presented our breakfast.

I took my knife, spread jam on my English muffin, and then pointed the red knife at Ray. "I'm pretty sure Tam True is out of the mansion on the hill. Can you find her?" I asked.

# CHAPTER 56

Tam True had fallen a long way since I had seen her on the porch of the mansion on the hill. She sat at a small table behind the H&R Grocery Store on Queen Street in Frederiksted. She had her head down on the table and was snoring gently. Her long black hair tumbled in a filthy heap, completely covering her head. She wore a torn, dirty white T-shirt several sizes too big and short, cut-off blue jeans.

Ray sat across from her and I stood to the side.

"Mrs. True," Ray said gently.

Her head raised, and she looked at us in a daze through bloodshot eyes. "What the fuck you want," she spat.

Ray shrugged, and she took her glare from Ray to me.

"You from the police," she said. "I remember you."

I nodded. "No."

"Can I buy you a beer," Ray asked.

"Fuck no," She said with venom, then she seemed to reconsider, "Rum," she said.

I turned away from the little courtyard and went into the store.

When I returned to the small courtyard, Tam True had pulled her unruly black hair into a ponytail and was sitting up straighter.

I handed her the glass of rum and coke, pulled a chair up, and joined Ray.

On the way to Frederiksted, we had decided that Ray would lead, and I would listen. This would be his interview.

"Why aren't you still at the mansion?" he asked.

She smiled a crooked smile and, with a cock of her head, said, "No money,"

Ray nodded.

She continued, "One day, checks are rolling in, and then that puke died, and the money quit." Anger grew in her voice, "I was his wife, and those pricks said I don't get any money, what the fuck!" she hissed and gulped the rum down, slamming the glass on the small table. Lowering her head and shaking it, she repeated, "What the fuck,"

"You killed the golden goose," Ray said.

She raised her head and looked Ray in the eye with a wicked stare, and her lips parted. "That prick gave me to his home boys,"

Ray stayed silent and raised his mirrored sunglasses, placing them on his short, white hair. His eyes were tired, and with his ever-present sunglasses off, I saw exhaustion mingled with sadness.

"What kind of an animal tells the pigs like that to have their way with his wife?"

Ray shook his head and, in a rare moment, reached across the table and covered her small, fragile hands with his huge hand.

We sat for a long while before she spoke.

"I knew he was a bad man, but all that money, the house, the cars," she said, looking up at Ray. Moisture started forming in her jet-black eyes.

"It was our wedding party, and he told those pigs they could have me," her eyes hardened, "He called me "his" whore."

We both sat silent.

She rubbed her arms and looked at me. I got up and went back for another rum.

When I got back, Ray still sat with his big hand over her small hands. I set the second rum and coke down and took my seat. She took a sip and said. "I didn't sleep all night. Those pigs left early, and I felt Sam get up. I laid there…" She paused and took another sip.

"I went to the window and looked out and saw him in the pool, just staring at the sunrise like he was some kind of a king or something."

"You went and got the gas," Ray said.

Her eyes froze on Ray hard in the harsh light of the courtyard. She nodded.

"And," he prompted.

Still staring into Ray's eyes, she said. "The pig didn't even know I was there. I set the gas can down and just let the gas flow. I stood up and watched the sun as it came over the rise. I can still smell the gas. The stupid fuck never even knew I was there." She paused, "Till I lit the gas," for the first time since we had sat down, she gave Ray a smile. Her straight white teeth flashed brightly, and then she said. "I'd never smelled burnt flesh before."

Ray nodded.

"Then the pricks told me no Sam, no money." She began to cry, "I had it all: money, respect, and power. I was rich, and I fucked it up."

"You killed the golden goose, Ray said.

She nodded and dropped her head to the table, sobbing.

I rose and walked back into the store. I pulled the tape recorder out of my pocket and checked it, and then I called Dory and FBI Agent Mike Farmer.

A small brown-skinned lady watched me from behind the old wooden counter. Her eyes were moist as she sat silently watching me.

I thought about what Tam True had said. I looked at the old woman and thought about the waves of evil and how they reached out and touched so many lives and turned those lives into evil. It was a living thing that I had been around for so long that it was beginning to push into the very pores of my soul.

I led Dory and Mike into the small courtroom, where Ray was still sitting, holding Tam True's hand. Ray looked up when we came in, and I knew he felt the sadness that was tearing at me.

Dory put his hand on Ray's shoulder and said. "We got this."

Ray nodded and got up.

As we walked out of the store, I could hear Dory reading Tam her rights. "*You have the right to be raped*," I thought as the bright afternoon sunlight slammed into my eyes.

Ray pulled his sunglasses off the top of his head and carefully wiped them on the bottom of his shirt. He put the glasses back on and the two mirrors again were staring at me, "You didn't tell them about Madge Thomas."

I shook my head.

"We need more evidence."

I nodded and said, "Right now, she's just a hunch. A damn good hunch but just a hunch"

Ray smiled, "So, Mad Dog, what now?"

"We investigate the shit out of her and figure this thing out," I said.

We were driving down Queen Mary Highway when the call came.

"Yo, Mad Dog, this is Antonio, Antonio Mendoza, we need to talk."

We were less than a mile from the side road that would take us to Mendoza's private drive. "I can be there in ten minutes," I said.

"Just pull in. The boys will be expecting you," he said and hung up.

The young guards in the bush had not moved and still sat watching us from their hiding places as we drove down the dirt road to the compound.

Kiki was standing in front of Mendoza's house when we pulled into the common area. They searched us again and then led us into the main house. Mendoza was sitting at his dining counter eating a sandwich when we came in. He motioned for us to sit.

We sat, and he pointed across the room at a tall, skinny black kid in a tattered tee shirt. "Marco, tell these men what you told me."

The boy looked at us. He was easily six feet eight inches tall, but I would have been surprised if he weighed one hundred forty pounds. He seemed to pull into himself when the gang leader spoke.

"Tell them," he said his mouth full of food.

The boy unfolded and rose to a stooped posture that still towered over Ray's huge frame. He shoved both his hands into his loose blue jeans, giving Mendoza a fearful glance. "I, "he stammered, "I mow lawns. "

Ray and I nodded, and we both sat at the counter across from Mendoza.

"I know a locked shed," he flicked a glance at Mendoza and continued, "I went into it," he paused, "through the window."

"Stealing," Ray said.

The boy flinched.

"Tell them," Mendoza said, seeming to lose patience.

"I saw the truck, the truck in the photos, I saw it."

"Where," I asked.

"I can take you," he said.

"How far?" Ray asked and stood.

The boy raised his hands and opened them both in front of him. His crooked black fingers were so long and his palms so small that they reminded me of crabs. "Ten miles," he said, looking fearfully through the crab-like fingers.

I looked at Mendoza, and he nodded, "Let's go," I said.

"Wait," Mendoza said," I'm tired of being cooped up here, I'm going."

Ray drove, and the boy rode shotgun while Mendoza and I sat in the back seat. The boy never spoke. He just pointed.

We followed Queen Mary back toward Christiansted about two miles and then turned down a narrow-paved road. In two more miles, the boy motioned for Ray to pull down a long, straight dirt road. The road had barbwire fences and goatherds on both sides. We drove for another three miles before the weather-ravaged shed came into view.

The shed was behind a gated fence, bush grew up around the sides and back of the shed and covered it in shadow.

I got out and inspected the gate. It was locked with an old paddle lock. I pulled my lock picks out and, in less than a minute, had the gate swung open. A path through the grass showed a vehicle had recently driven up to the shed.

Ray pulled through the gate, and the four of us approached the shed's front doors. I pulled my picks out and attacked the cheap paddle lock. The lock popped in seconds, and I swung the ancient wooden doors open, allowing the bright sun to pour into the dark dusty shed.

The first thing I saw was the old license plate, "FISH M."

"Bingo," Ray said as we stared at the truck.

I walked to the front of the truck and examined the bumper.

"Ray," I said.

He and Mendoza came around the truck, and I pointed at the inch-long shred of bloody cloth hanging from the bumper.

"I'm betting that's a small piece of Steve Whistler," Ray said.

"Yep," I said, "Let's get out of here. I don't want to spook the killer,"

We all moved out of the shed, and I locked it.

"We need to find out who owns this shed," I said.

"Nope," Ray said.

I looked over at him, and he pointed.

Across the long goat-filled field stood a neat-looking yellow house. The small patio in the back, the large breadfruit tree, and the garden—we were looking at the back of Madge Thomas's home.

"Shit," I said.

"What," Mendoza said.

"Just a thought," I said, moving back toward the truck, "we need to go."

Mendoza looked at the kid and said, "You done good, Lurch,"

For the first time since I had met him, the boy stretched to his full height and smiled.

Mendoza pulled a bundle of bills from his pocket and peeled a twenty-dollar bill from the wad. He handed the boy the money, and it disappeared into the pockets of his loose-fitting blue jeans.

"What now?" Mendoza said.

"Now we'll take you two back to the compound and do some serious investigating," Ray said.

"I want in on this," Mendoza said, "this prick has been haunting me, and I want in on the kill."

Ray looked back at me and then said, "You got it."

Mendoza sat back in his seat beside me and gave me a small thumbs-up. The gesture was odd, coming from a man I suspected was himself an accomplished serial killer.

Ray and I didn't speak until we had dropped Mendoza and the boy he called Lurch off.  As we sped back down the compound road, Ray said, "We got her."

I nodded and called Dory and Mike for the second time in three hours.

When I called, the FBI agent and Dory were both at the VIPD headquarters in Frederiksted. We agreed to meet at the headquarters.

Ray and I came into the main office and the uniformed officer at the main desk called Dory. "He said for you to come around to the side door, and he'll let you in," the officer said, pointing to the side of the building. As Ray and I walked down the side of the building, Mike opened the side door and ushered us in. "Dory and I just got a second statement, and he's booking her," Mike said.

"Got a coffee while we wait?" Ray said.

Mike left us standing in the hall and went into the room marked "investigations." A few minutes later, he came out with two Styrofoam cups of coffee. "Dory should be done in just a few minutes," he said, "The girl gave a full confession."

Ray shook his head, "What do you think they'll do."

Mike shrugged, "Charge her murder one and plead her to manslaughter."

"Yeah," Ray said, "if the home boys don't get to her first."

That little thought left us all quiet till Dory appeared at the end of the hall.

"I got us a conference room. You mind if the chief and AG sit in on this little meeting?"

"No," Farmer said. I've got the U.S. attorney coming over. Can we wait for him?"

"Sure," Dory said.

Dory and Farmer walked ahead of us and as they went around the corner, I whispered, "VIPD and Feds working together?"

"Fucking weird," Ray said, raising his sunglasses for a second for emphasis.

I had to smile.

It was almost an hour before the meeting started.

Cheri showed up about fifteen minutes before the U.S. Attorney Tom Green and the Chief insisted we not only sit in on the meeting but invited us to participate in the conversation.

Cheri and I went out to get a cup of coffee while we waited for Green, and she said, "This is weird. The Feds and Locals never work together, and civilians like us are never welcome."

"It's simple," Ray said, "the Feds really want and need a feather in their cap, and a big serial killer case is about the biggest feather you can get, and the Territory wants money."

"Money?" I asked.

"Fuck, man, all the StreGo owners are from here. The money flowing into the islands makes this one of the biggest tax revenues in Virgin Island history." Ray said, patting his front pocket. "You don't think the Governor doesn't get cranky when tax revenue like that is fleeing the islands like rats fleeing a sinking ship."

"But why us?" I asked.

"Simple, we're solving the case." He said.

"Plus, Ziggy is now about to be worth millions, and if he wants us on this, we're on this," Cheri said.

I saw Tom Green and Mike Farmer walking down the hall. "Let's go do this," I said.

The meeting started with us sharing everything we had on the case that pointed toward Thomas being the killer.

The U.S. attorney and Kip Richards from the Attorney General's office asked questions they would need to get arrest and search warrants. They agreed that a search warrant based on Lurch's statement that he saw the truck and Tim's video of the hit-and-run would give the AG a Territorial warrant to search the shed.

We took a break while Kip called the AG's office and dictated a search warrant.

As the next part of the meeting progressed, all the parties agreed that the hit and run could be separate from the list of serial killings and tried in the Territorial court. The six killings involving the small caliber handgun that Cooper, the ballistic expert, had tied together would be the core of the federal case.

Everyone agreed that the shed search should be followed immediately by the search of Thomas's house and vehicles. The probable cause statement for the shed would be identical to the probable cause statement for the house, except a paragraph would be added to point out what objects were found to support probable cause in the shed search.

Both arrest warrants would be simultaneous and include all information from both searches.

The chief and the US attorney argued over the language for the press release for thirty minutes while we waited for the warrant on the shed. It was five o'clock in the evening when the VIPD detective called with the signed warrant. Dory and Mike went out the door and headed for the shed while Ray, Cheri, and I were left sitting on our hands.

# CHAPTER 58

The call was short and concise. "They're on to you," the voice said. "Madge Thomas."

"Who?" She said, taking a quick look out the window.

The caller had already hung up.

Madge looked at her watch. It was three thirty in the afternoon. She finished the sandwich she was eating and got to work.

Madge knew this time would come. It took her ten minutes to prepare the house.

Everything she needed was in the back of her escape vehicle. She opened her back door and looked around. Nothing. She moved toward the cover of the big breadfruit tree and then began to glide through the shadows of the fruit trees that lined her property.

She stopped and looked back at the little yellow house, and a pang of sadness coursed through her.

One block away, the two officers who had been assigned to watch the house were admiring a fifteen-year-old girl sunbathing in her yard. They never saw Madge leave, and she never saw them. That was a lucky thing for everyone.

By four o'clock, Madge Thomas was in her blacked-out gray Ford Explorer headed for her "hideout."

The game had changed. It was now far more interesting. She wondered how they had found her. The detectives, she guessed, and the thought made her smile; she loved a good challenge, advisories worthy of respect.

She thought back over the years. The young boy in Mutual Homes that had got her started. He had held her little sister down and raped her. It had taken Madge weeks to get her sister to tell the story, and then it had taken Madge months to trap the little bastard and kill him. She still remembered the feeling of watching his wicked little rapist's eyes go glassy as the knife did its work. It had been years of peace then. The marriage to Mike, the birth of Charlie, and her first kill seemed more like a dream than reality. All that stopped the day she caught Mike with Charlie. The boy had been maybe seven, and the man she loved was molesting him. She had waited till he was going fishing by himself and asked to go. It had been so simple to loop the line over his foot as he launched the fish trap and give him a little push. No scream, no conversation, just that pervert son of a bitch sinking to the bottom of the ocean.

For her, the police force had been natural, more money for her and Charlie and an endless list of pieces of shit that needed killing. The goat field behind the house had become rich in the fertilizer of the wicked. Over the years, she had quit counting, quit caring how many she had killed. They had all been the wicked that ripped the guts out of her island. She wondered if they would find her field of the wicked. Of course, they would. They would have to look for Terry Jeffery, and he was planted with the rest.

What would people think when they knew the truth? Would she be an island hero or a monster? No matter, she was what she was, and her whole life had been about making hard decisions. She would go on as long as she could. She thought of the detectives. They had a history of slashing out the island's evil. They were kindred souls, and if they got in the way, she would kill them.

After a good night's sleep, she would listen to the news and figure out what had happened. Then, she would put her trophies on her new wall and go back to work. There was an endless hoard of StreGo owners, and she was going to kill them all.

# CHAPTER 59

It had been nearly forty hours since I had slept, and when I lay down in our bed at the safe house, I was gone. My dreams were bad, but when I woke, none of them stayed with me. When I walked into the front room, everyone was huddled around the TV. "What's up?" I asked as I moved toward the TV. A commercial about shampoo was on.

Cheri looked up at me, tears streaming from her eyes. She rose, came over, and hugged me.

"What's going on?" I asked.

Cheri spoke in a choked voice. "Thomas wired her house."

"What?" I asked.

"The bitch wired the house with high explosives, and when they kicked the door, it blew," Ray said.

"Who?" I asked.

"We don't know. They have some video on the TV, but it's mostly of the house, and we can't get anyone to call us back." John said. He was sitting at a desk he had set up, his eyes fixed on the eight monitors that watched the property around our safe house.

"Is she coming after us?" I asked, looking at John.

He shrugged his shoulders.

An agonizing hour later, Dory called. He and Farmer were OK, but six swat members had been hospitalized, and two had been killed. He promised to call back and we sat around the big great room. I spent most of my time looking out the window and wondering what I had done wrong. Cheri busied herself cleaning and cooking. Tim spent hours trying to clean up videos that we didn't need because we knew who the killer was, but no one told him to stop because we were all dealing with the shock in our own way. John hovered over his monitors and, every hour took his assault rifle and made a sweep over the property. Ray got drunk and then took a nap. The getting drunk sounded like a good idea, but I knew it was a bad idea.

Ziggy called just after noon, and Cheri put him on speakerphone.

"Kind of a cluster fuck down there," he said.

"Yeah," I said, "you, OK?"

"Yeah, I'm alive and living at Club FBI."

"Lots of chicks and Margaritas at Club FBI?" Ray asked fresh from his nap and opening a new beer.

"No chicks and no blender, but I do have a good supply of Miller Lite."

"How's StreGo doing?" I asked.

"Amazing, my checks for my percentage came in…." Ziggy stopped, "not a good subject, hah," he said.

"Nope," I said, "any idea who put the ad in the paper?"

"Yep," he said. "The agent working that side of the case called me yesterday. Its Tom Severs. He doesn't have any takers, but he should have plenty of cash if anyone wants to sell."

"What proof, did the agent say?" I asked.

Ziggy said, "Fingerprints on the inside of the envelope and DNA where he licked the stamp."

I laughed, "Not a very smart cop."

"Too many steroids," Ziggy said.

We shared a little small talk, and he told me we were still on the payroll. Ray told him to demand a blender and female companionship, and we hung up.

Around three o'clock, Tim said, "Hey guys, come look at this."

We all moved over to the computer he had been working on. When Charlie was born, the name on the birth certificate of their father was Mike Jones. That truck was registered to Mike Jones."

"OK," Cheri said, "so we know that Thomas's husband or spouse and Charlie's dad was Mike Jones."

"Mike Jones, DOB March 21, 1964," Tim said. "I ran Mr. Jones through the VI tax system."

"How?" Ray asked.

Tim gave Ray a sly smile, "Let's just say the territory has a rather poor firewall."

"Shit," Cheri said, "you're hacking the VI government computers?"

"You want to know what I found or not?" Tim asked.

"Shit, yes," Ray said, sliding closer.

"OK," Tim said running his hands over the keys, "Mike Jones has been paying tax on a piece of property by Altona Lagoon."

"Altona Lagoon?" I said. "I know where the lagoon is, but I didn't know of any houses there."

A Google Earth picture popped up, and Tim pointed at four structures on the southwest edge of the Lagoon. "I'm fairly sure that this house here, is Mike Jones's house," he tapped the map.

"That's some serious bush," Ray said.

The house was set on a piece of property that could be entered from one road. The property backed the lagoon.

"See these boats?" Ray said. There must be a path through the bush so the person who lives there can pull these skiffs down to the lagoon.

I studied the photo, and Ray was right; at a point in the house's open yard, there were two small boats. "You're probably right," I said.

"You think she's there?" John asked.

"Maybe," Tim said, "someone is paying the taxes, and the property looks like someone takes care of it, so maybe."

"She's a security freak, and now we know she plants booby traps; going in there will be way tricky. That bush is thick on all sides. The ways in are limited and easy to put surveillance on and booby trap." John said.

"We could sit on it and see if she comes out?" Tim said.

"What's this, "we," Cheri said, "You got a mouse in your pocket."

"I want in," Tim said. "I want to go with you, I'm tired of just looking at the computer while you guys have all the fun."

"Let the kid go," John said, "I'll keep him out of trouble."

"You can't even keep yourself out of trouble," Cheri said.

"He can go." I said, "Just for the surveillance part, we'll need two surveillance groups, and having a fifth body will help."

I pointed at the house. "We will need a group to watch the water exit and the land exit," I said. "The guys watching the water exit will need three people, two on the water and one in a truck at the lagoon to follow her if she goes out that way."

"First things first, Cheri, call Mr. Ramsey and see if he will take you up in his helicopter to get photos. He flies up and down the north shore all the time and shouldn't raise any red flags." I said.

Cheri walked over toward the kitchen to make her call.

"Ray, you, and John find a flat boat and go into the lagoon and cover the water exit. Tim, I want you parked in a vehicle at the lagoon. If Thomas is in there and she comes out, you will have to follow her until the rest of us can catch up. You up to that?"

"Yeah, I get a gun?" Tim asked.

"NO!" John, Ray, and I all said in unison.

"What are we going to tell Farmer and Dory?" Ray asked.

"Nothing," I said, "If we get an ID, we will call them in to make the arrest."

"All we're going to be doing," Cheri said, returning from the phone call, "is seeing if this lead is accurate. As soon as we spot her, we try to follow her and call in Calvary."

"That's the plan," I said.

# CHAPTER 60

Cheri and John went to the parking lot at the Yacht Club, where Tony Ramsey, a local businessman, had agreed to pick them up in his small helicopter. It was six thirty when they returned, and Tim downloaded the digital photos and videos they had taken during their two passes over the property by Altona Lagoon.

"This is great stuff," Tim said as he began scanning the first photos he had on the computer.

The photo clearly showed the house on the tax property. The windows were boarded up, and the roof appeared to be badly damaged. A black SUV was parked in front of the house.

"Doesn't look occupied, but someone is there," Tim said.

"We didn't see anyone, but you're right. The SUV doesn't show any dust or anything. It hasn't been there long, and if you look at the second pass photos, you can see that the plywood covering on the front doors is pulled off."

"Best bet is someone is there then," I said.

"Tim, on the second pass, I think we got a pretty good shot of the SUV's license. Can you run it?" Cheri asked.

Tim moved through the photos until Cheri told him to stop and a photo of the SUV and the front of the house.

"There, Tim," Cheri said, pointing, "That's the best photo."

Tim manipulated the photo and zoomed in on the license plate on the front of the SUV.

I read the plate and said, "Ray, can you call Dory and have him run that plate?"

"No need," Tim said, as he punched a set of keys and said, "The plate is registered to StreGo."

"This hacking has got to stop," Cheri said, staring at the screen that clearly said "Virgin Islands Department of Motor Vehicles."

"Look," John said, pointing at the screen.

"What," Tim said.

John moved his finger to the screen and pointed to the partly open door. Toward the bottom of the door was a black object.

Tim zoomed in on the object till it filled the screen. "Great focus," he said as what appeared to be the barrel of a gun appeared on the screen.

"Call Mike and Dory, Tim, and tell them right where the property is. Tell them she is armed and dangerous," Cheri said, rising.

The entire room was in motion, "John, you're with Cheri. Go to the lagoon. Ray, you, and I are going to the road to the house and blocking it till the calvary comes. Tim, you have to get them to the road and the lagoon. Tell Mike Farmer everything and tell him to hurry. If the chopper spooked her, she may already be gone or getting ready to go, and we can't lose her"

Tim rose and said, "I want to go."

"No," I said sharply, pointing at him, "I need you here to act like a command center. Do you understand?"

Tim nodded.

Ray came out of the back room with two large canvas bags and threw a flak jacket at me. "Time to go, " he said.

Ray and I ran out and piled into his SUV. He spun a cookie in the mansion's parking lot and then sped down the drive. Cheri and John were right behind us as we sped down the South Side Road.

I dug into the black duffel bag and pulled out two hand radios. I turned one on and tuned it to 72. "Are you there?" I asked.

John answered, "Blue Dog, this is Red Rover. I have you."

Ray took his eyes off the road and glanced at me. "Red Rover? John said. That big dumb fucker is crazy."

"How about Dog and something else?" I said on the radio.

"I want to be Red Rover, over," the radio squawked.

"Let me know when you're at the lagoon," I said as my cell phone buzzed.

"I'm on my way," Mike Farmer said, and I could hear the roar of engines in the background.

We crossed over the island to the north side and sped west toward the road that turned into the house. I could hear the sound of distant sirens.

We pulled up the road into the Altona area and slowed. Cheri and John passed us, and Red Rover radioed to say they were setting up in the lagoon's parking lot.

We had just parked Ray's SUV when the three black federal Ford Explorers stopped across from us. Mike Farmer, dressed in a suit and flak jacket, jumped out of the lead SUV with a wicked-looking assault rifle. Seven men in black SWAT suits poured out of the SUV and ran over to the head of the road. The sirens were getting louder by the second.

"You five," Farmer said, pointing down the road. "Down that road and secure it, no one in, no one out." The men hurried out of sight.

Farmer turned to me, "You sure it's her?"

"That's my best guess," I said.

"Shit," he said as the first VIPD patrol cars arrived. "This is going to be a circus."

Tom Sever and his partner climbed out of the patrol car. They both carried the standard-issue riot guns. Tom looked at Farmer and then at me. "Where do you want us?" he asked me.

"I have five men up the road," Farmer said. "Just stay here till I can talk to your people."

"Done," Sever said and moved with his partner back behind Ray's SUV.

Three more patrol cars were pulling up to the side of the road when the first shots began to ring out.

Mike's radio barked," Officer down, officer down!"

Mike keyed his radio and said, "Pull back."

Seconds later, one of the black-suited agents emerged at the head of the road carrying a second agent.

I heard Sever behind me notifying his commander of the shots fired and requesting medical support.

Ray and I both pulled our guns and moved back behind the SUV.

"What a fucking mess," Ray said as we stooped behind the SUV.

I watched as one of the FBI agents set the wounded man behind our SUV and began to administer first aid.

"Hit in the leg," I said as a second volley of shots erupted from the bush. I looked up and realized we were losing the daylight quickly. The road was already starting to fall into shadows.

I heard a man scream and then three more shots. I saw movement behind me, and Tom Sever and his partner melted into the bush. "Stop!" I yelled, but the officers had disappeared.

"These idiots are going to be shooting at each other in a few seconds," Ray said.

My radio barked. "Dog, Dog, come in, Dog."

"Yeah," I answered, "Just use cell phones," I said, turning the radio off and stuffing it in its pouch.

My cell rang, "We heard shots." Cheri said.

"Yeah, someone shot one of the FBI guys; it looks like he's OK, they have medical coming, but there are still at least three FBI and two VIPD in the bush by the front road."

"Where are you," She asked.

"We're hunkered down and safe," I said, looking at Ray, who had taken off his sunglasses in the dimming light and was adjusting the straps to his bulletproof vest.

"There are two FBI vehicles and three patrol cars in the parking lot here. They seem to be setting up a parameter, so John and I are pulling back. I think we should let the cops handle this."

I heard two more shots, one of them a shotgun. I looked over as a bullet tore into the black SUV that Agent Farmer had arrived in.

Ray and I both looked at the nice new hole in the SUV. "gotta go? " I said and hung up.

"Shall we let the cops…." I began to ask when a black-clad figure charged out of the bush behind our vehicle, crossed the road, and dove into the bush across the road.

"See that," I said.

"What?" Ray asked.

I pointed up the hill where the figure had dove into the bush.

"What?" Ray repeated, his voice nearly drowned out by the loud approach of multiple sirens.

"It was her," I said, pointing at the bush on the far side of the road where the black-clad figure had disappeared.

I looked around for any of the officers or agents, but they were all crouched down like us behind various vehicles. I realized that we were parked the furthest east of the vehicles. Madge Thomas had flanked everyone and was making her escape.

In a crouch, I ran toward the bush where the black figure had disappeared.

"What the fuck you doing," I heard Ray say from behind me.

I didn't respond but instead plunged into the bush, where I saw the person, I was convinced was ex-VIPD Detective Sergeant Madge Thomas.

When I breached the bush, I stopped and listened. Ahead of me, I heard a crash and branches breaking. I started to run toward the sound. The bush was getting dark in the dusky light, and I pushed my way through the lightly spaced Tan Tan bush. The bush's thorns ripped at my arm and clothing, but I could see where the dark figure was pushing through the bush and following the path. I heard a distinct slashing sound and, at the same time, saw a cleanly cut, one-inch-thick branch. If it was Thomas, she had a machete and was hacking her way through the bush. As she hacked away in front of me, she was leaving an easy trail through the bush to follow.

"Dog," A voice said behind me.

"Ray?" I looked behind me and Ray came through the cut in the bush. He was carrying his big 44 revolver. I held my finger to my lip and said, "She's ahead." In the quiet I could hear the hacking of the machete.

"What the fuck are you waiting for," Ray whispered and charged ahead of me into the freshly cut path.

The bush was getting darker and harder to see by the second. The sun had set and the dusk light no longer penetrated the deep cover of the bush. It was all I could do not to get distracted and separated from Ray. I wanted to tell the big man to slow down but knew he wouldn't. I fought to keep up.

I saw a blink of light in the bush in front of us and realized that Thomas had a flashlight. I imagined her with a flashlight in one hand and a machete in the other, hacking her way to freedom. I tried to envision what was on the other side of the bush. "She's going to the elementary school," I said.

Ray just kept forging ahead. I looked to the left and saw the eight-foot cyclone fence only about ten feet from where we were plunging through the bush. Ray was too far ahead. I veered toward the fence and pushed through the heavy bush. The fence was covered with thorn bush and topped with two strands of barbwire.

I tore my bulletproof vest off and threw it over the fence. I then did my fat old man climb over the big fence trick. It wasn't pretty but with a lot of whispered cussing and a few scratches, I fell to the cleared field that surrounded the elementary school. In the far distance ahead of me I heard the chopping of machete. I ran up the fence line.

Forty yards ahead of me, I saw a rifle clatter to the ground, and then a black-clad figure began to climb over the fence. I waited for the figure to drop to the ground before I spoke.

"Stop!" I yelled.

The figure froze and turned toward me.

"Stop!" I repeated.

Madge Thomas's right hand was a blur as she drew the pistol at her hip and began to raise it.

I fired, and from the bush, a cannon roared. Like a doll, her body was slammed to my left, and then back in a slow arching spin; she thudded to the ground hard.

"Bulletproof vest," Ray yelled from the darkness on the far side of the fence.

I leveled my Glock on her head and crabbed forward till I stood over her. She was face down in the fetal position with a small caliber pistol still tight in her right hand. I stepped hard on her wrist and the pistol came loose. Ray appeared at the other side of the fence and pointed the big revolver at the still body.

"Got any cuffs," I asked keeping my eye on Thomas.

"I'm not a fucking cop; what am I gonna do with handcuffs," Ray said.

## Epilogue

The search of the house on the lagoon had been a horror story. In a suitcase, the FBI agents found evidence and mementos from dozens of murders dating back to when Madge Thomas had been a teen.

Madge Thomas was placed into federal custody for multiple murders. She never made a statement or explained her actions. Three days after her arrest while in detention at the Golden Grove Detention Center, she was hacked to death by a sixteen-year-old inmate from Antonio Mendoza housing development.

Tam True pleaded guilty to manslaughter and was sentenced to two years of incarceration by a judge I later learned was her second cousin.

Mike Ziggler took all his money and left the island. He is now living on a private island in Thailand. He left our little group paid in full, plus a nice bonus.

# The End

To my readers,

Thank you for allowing me to share The Strength of St. Croix.

I want to thank the hundreds of people who have supported me during the development of the St. Croix Mystery Series. You know who you are.

Like all writers, I draw on the experiences and the people of my life to build my stories. Although all the characters in this book are fictional, many are drawn in part from some of the wonderful real-life characters in my life both friend and foe.

I want to thank the amazing people of St. Croix. In the years Charlene, my wife, and I had the pleasure of living on the Island, we were blessed with enough friends and rich experiences to last a lifetime and fill a hundred books.

I tip my hat to the amazing Island of St. Croix, where you can still watch a green flash at sunset while you listen to live jazz and sip your Dark and Diet.